"Deliciously deviant . . . Akin to
— *Library Journal* (Starred Revi

Mona Lisa St. James made a deat
would do anything to save her mother s art gallery. Unfortu
nately, not only is The Red painted red, but it's in the red.

Just as she realizes she has no choice but to sell it, a mysterious man comes in after closing time and makes her an
offer: He will save The Red if she agrees to submit to him for
the period of one year.

The man is handsome, English, and terribly tempting...but
surely her mother didn't mean for Mona to sell herself to a
stranger. Then again, she did promise to do anything to save
The Red . . .

The Red is a novel of erotic fantasy from Tiffany Reisz,
USA Today bestselling author of *The Bourbon Thief* and the
Original Sinners series.

Trade Paperback ISBN: 978-1949769296 (8th Circle Press)

Library Hardcover ISBN: 978-1949769036 (8th Circle Press)

MP3 CD Audiobook ISBN: 978-1541459052 (Tantor Audio)

CD Audiobook ISBN: 978-1541409057 (Tantor Audio)

Cover design by Andrew Shaffer

Front and back cover images used under license from Shutterstock.com

www.8thcirclepress.com

First Edition

THE RED

AN EROTIC FANTASY

TIFFANY REISZ

CONTENTS

To the Mistress

I: THE FOX HUNT

*I*t had always been called The Red Gallery, even before the gallery was red.

Originally it was called Red's because a man named Red owned the place and for no other reason. Mona's mother, however, said the name came from the 1920s when The Red was a speakeasy. So many people were killed during bloody gangster shootouts, she said, that the place had been nick-named The Little Red Shooting Gallery. None of that was true, of course, but Mona's mother had been the sort of woman who valued beauty over truth. She loved The Red Gallery and thought it deserved the very best origin story. Mona never passed on that fiction herself, but she never denied it either. She also kept the brick painted crimson and her own brown hair colored candy apple red.

It's what her mother would have wanted.

Her mother had loved The Red Gallery so very much that her last words to Mona had been, "Do anything you have to, but save The Red." And for that reason alone Mona sat at her desk in The Red Gallery long past closing time, adding up numbers again and again in the hopes of finding a misplaced

1

zero somewhere, a zero that would turn assets of fifty thousand dollars into five hundred thousand dollars. She'd robbed Peter to pay Paul and now Peter was at the door and pounding. There was no one left to rob to pay him.

Unless she sold the gallery.

Why her mother loved this place so much Mona might never know. Oh, Mona loved The Red too, their little gallery on Savoy Street. She loved its painted red brick and glass storefront, the ebony-stained hardwood, the red velvet curtains along the walls that made the colors of the canvases pop like balloons. She loved the little office off the main gallery that had once been her mother's but was now hers. She loved the storage room in the back where all the paintings and sculptures not currently on display were safely kept —a second private art gallery. What she didn't love was the debt. If her mother had died a quick death, Mona might have been able to save the gallery. But she hadn't. She'd been sick and had lingered for two years, getting a little better and then a little worse, better, then worse, a step forward, a fall back. In the end, all she could leave Mona was the deed to the gallery and a fortune in medical debt that her mother's life insurance barely touched.

And no one gave a damn about art anymore.

She knew that wasn't true, but all attempts to revitalize the gallery had failed. Up and coming artists had drawn young hip crowds. But while the hip young crowds were happy to drink the free wine and eat the free crackers and cheese, they didn't buy the paintings. Older artists had flooded the markets with their works and were selling for peanuts, if they were selling at all. She'd tried to entice the estate of a recently deceased painter to give her the exhibition of his collection, but they'd gone with a bigger gallery uptown. She didn't blame them. She might not have picked The Red Gallery either.

2

Today, she'd let go the very last member of her staff.

Except for Tou-Tou, of course. She'd never let go of Tou-Tou.

"Don't worry," she said to the little black cat curled up in the corner of her office in his bed. "If I sell the gallery, you won't be homeless. You can come live with me."

Tou-Tou—short for Toulouse-Lautrec—merely glanced in her direction, blinking his luminescent green eyes before returning to the task at hand, namely licking his right paw for the next ten minutes. Tou-Tou had been the gallery cat for ten years. Her mother had found the malnourished black kitten in an alley two streets away and had brought him here to nurse him back to health. He'd never gotten very big, but his coat was glossy and soft, his eyes bright, and his purrs loud enough to wake the dead. She wasn't allowed pets in her apartment, but what her landlady didn't know wouldn't hurt her. Ten years. Mona had been fifteen when they found Tou-Tou. Ten years. Ten years ago the gallery had been the apple of Savoy Street, the darling of the art district. But rents had gotten too high and the galleries, one by one, had shut their doors or moved. Only The Red was left behind.

And now it would close its doors too.

Mona rose from her desk and walked to Tou-Tou's bed. She stroked his head, his chin, pressed her hand to his side to feel that marvelous diesel engine purr. It comforted her. She whispered promises to Tou-Tou, that he would like it at her apartment. That she wasn't firing him, she was selling the gallery. She told him to tell her mother—her mother had been certain cats could communicate with the dead—that Mona had done all she could to save The Red. No banks would loan her money. The credit cards were maxed. Bankruptcy was imminent. Art for art's sake was a lovely idea in theory.

But art alone couldn't pay the bills.

3

Mona stood up straight and squared her shoulders. The wall clock said it was almost midnight. Sometime in the last hour she'd made up her mind to sell. She felt better now that she'd acknowledged she had no choice but to sell. The numbers weren't going to magically multiply no matter how long she stared at them. Might as well give up, go home, and sleep. She slung her black bag over her shoulder, took her red coat off the hook and laid it over her arm, slipped her feet back into her black heels and blew a goodnight kiss at Tou-Tou. Time to lock up. Time to give up. Except…

There was a man standing in the gallery.

Mona gasped, her hand over her mouth. It didn't seem he had heard her gasp. He didn't even turn to look at her. She swallowed hard, her heart running like the White Rabbit. He was tall and broad-shouldered and wore a three-piece black suit. He had one hand on his hip, one hand on his chin. Although his clothes were modern and he looked about forty years old, there was something about him that looked…old. No, not old. Old World, perhaps. Yes, that. Old World. She could think of no other way to describe him. It was the hair. That was it. He wore his hair in a style that would have best belonged on a Regency-era lord. Black and tousled, rakish even, he reminded her of Eugene Delacroix's dashing self-portraits. Dark eyes, black heart. To Mona he looked like the devil gone courting.

But who was the devil's lucky lady?

"Sir?" Mona finally worked up her courage to speak. "The gallery is closed."

He didn't speak at first. But he did move at last. He dropped his hand from his chin and stepped toward the small painting in front of him. It was a George Morland, a contemporary of Joshua Reynolds. Nothing terribly impressive about it. Merely an uninspired painting of men in red coats on horseback. A pretty painting, pretty and unobtrusive. Mona imagined an older couple looking to decorate a country house would take a shine to it. All it had done in the four months it hung on the gallery wall was gather dust.

"Things aren't what they seem."

His accent was English. She'd recognized those lovely vowels at once.

"No," she said. "I imagine they aren't."

"I hear your gallery is closing," he said. Again the right hand came to his chin, the left hand to his hip. The left hand drew her gaze. He was lean and the well-tailored vest emphasized his trim waist and hips. She was finding it very difficult not to enjoy looking at his body. The man was a work of art.

"*Closed*, I said. I told you the gallery is *closed*. It's almost midnight."

"You're in the red."

"So are you. That's the name of the gallery."

At that he turned and looked at her, met her eyes, smiled. She felt a current of fear run through her body, electric and exciting. Why hadn't she dressed better today? She wore her plain tweed skirt, her plain black blouse, and plain black heels. She looked more like a secretary than a gallery owner. If only—secretaries made far more money than she did these days.

"You're in the red," he said again. "In debt, I mean."

"What have you heard?" she asked. She knew local real estate developers could be aggressive when it came to prime property in prime locations. Had someone sent this man to force her to sell?

"I heard the gallery was in distress. Such a shame," he said. "It's a treasure trove."

"It's a money pit," she said.

He arched an eyebrow at her. He looked even more like the devil than ever. A dashing devil. Despite her fear, she

5

liked looking at him. He didn't seem dangerous. No, he seemed terribly dangerous. But he didn't seem violent. There was a difference.

"How so?" he asked.

"My mother bought paintings she couldn't re-sell," Mona said. "She spent huge sums of money on gallery parties that brought in no revenue. And she died of cancer last autumn. The bills were enormous."

"No father to help?"

"I don't know who my father is. My mother was a bohemian type."

"And you have no money?"

"Having no money right now would be a blessing because currently I have negative five hundred thousand dollars," she said. "So unless you're going to buy that Morland for five hundred thousand dollars, I'm afraid I'll have to ask you to leave. The gallery is closed, but it isn't closing—not yet. If you want to come back, you can. We'll open at ten tomorrow morning."

"It's not a Morland," he said.

"What?"

"I told you—things aren't always as they seem. There are machines for seeing through paint? Or am I mistaken?"

"X-ray machines?"

"Yes, those." He nodded sagely. "You should take this painting and have it run through one of those machines. Tell me what you see."

"I don't have one here," she said. "I'd have to find one."

"Do that. I'll return in one week," he said. "I want you to trust me."

"Why?"

"Because I would like to help you. I would like to help you very much indeed. But I can't help you if you don't trust me.

And I certainly can't help you if you sell the gallery. So do as I say."

"Do as you say?" She was flabbergasted. The gall of this man.

"You won't regret it," he said. "I assure you, you won't regret any of it, Mona."

"How do you know my name?"

"Mona Lisa St. James. You own The Red Gallery."

"Have you been stalking me?"

"Only watching," he said.

"You're scaring me."

"I can't help that," he said. "Although I do apologize. I will not harm you in any way. I hope you believe that."

She wanted to believe it.

"It would help if you told me how you got in without me hearing. The door was locked."

"Your mother had a spare key made. She hid it in the potted plant outside."

"What Mother lacked in common sense she made up for in style."

"That she did. Do you, by any chance, have a book of Morland's paintings?"

"I think so."

"Fetch it please."

"Fetch it?" Was she a dog now?

The man grinned that fiendish grin again. "Please."

Mad as it was, Mona returned to her office to find the book. It was on the shelf somewhere with hundreds of other art books her mother had collected through the years. They'd all have to be sold to a book collector, though it broke her heart to think of parting with them. After a few minutes searching, she found the slim blue Morland catalog and returned to the gallery.

The man was gone.

There was a bell on the door that chimed when anyone came or left. Her ears were trained to hear that bell no matter if she were in the office, the bathroom, or the back room. That bell meant a customer had entered and a customer meant money. But the bell hadn't rung and yet he was not there, not anywhere in the gallery. Nowhere at all.

Unbelievable. All of it. Yet the man's certainty had infected her somehow. Not a Morland he said. Not a Morland. Well, this book had a picture of every Morland ever catalogued.

She flipped through it, page after page, looking for the painting of the four men in red coats, the four brown horses. There. It *was* a Morland. Red coats. Brown horses. She examined the artist's signature in the book and found it matched the artist's signature on the painting.

The man in the suit was wrong.

And yet.

Mona lightly touched the signature—the ornate *M*, the curving *D*. She knew she shouldn't. One should never touch a painting with bare hands, but the painting was so uninteresting and uninspired and was taking up valuable wall space that she didn't feel too guilty about touching a tiny corner of it with her fingertip.

"Shit." The *M* flaked off onto her finger. Just like that. Barely a touch and the paint crumbled. Well, it was her fault and she'd take the blame for it when the painting's owner demanded an explanation for the damage. It could be repaired, but that meant more time and more money, money she didn't have. She peered at the bare spot where the *M* had been, fearful of seeing more damage. But she didn't see any damage.

She saw a *J*.

There was no *J* in Morland. But that was without a doubt the letter *J*.

Before she could stop herself, she'd used her red finger-nail to chip off one more tiny fleck of paint. It was against every rule. It was madness. But she did it anyway. She'd seen a glint of gold in the bottom of a box of China dishes and she was breaking the China to pieces to get to the gold.

And there it was.

An *R* after the *J*.

Mona took the painting off the wall, back to the office, flicked on the lights and as slowly and carefully as she could, set about extracting the top layer of paint off the signature below it. Her mother had taught her how to do it while simultaneously warning her never to do it. Yet her mother was gone and Mona did it. And when she finished, she not only had a *J* and an *R*. She'd uncovered an *E* and possibly a *Y* as well.

J.

J. Reynolds.

Joshua Reynolds?

Surely not. Or was it? She had to find out.

"Forgive me, Mother," Mona breathed as she went about removing more of the paint.

Her mother had told her to do anything to save the gallery. That's exactly what Mona would do.

II: THE COURTESAN

*T*he week passed in a blur as the newly discovered Reynolds painting became the talk of the art world. Mona spent hours on the phone with arts and culture reporters who'd seized upon the story in a slow news week. They all wanted to know how she knew there was a Reynolds hidden under the unremarkable Morland painting. All she could tell them was that a visitor to the gallery noted something off about the painting. When she examined the signature, she noticed the flaking paint and followed a hunch. When they wanted to know the visitor's name to talk to him as well, she had to tell them the truth—she had no idea who he was. He came in, made a comment about the painting and left before she could get his name. The news drew visitors to the gallery. She sold two pieces for ten thousand each.

All thanks to the mysterious man in the three-piece suit.

She'd almost forgotten he'd promised to return in a week. But on the seventh evening she remembered and lingered long at her desk after the gallery had closed. She listened for the bell as she did her paperwork. She never heard it ring.

But at five to midnight, Tou-Tou hopped out of his basket and ran through the door to the gallery as if he'd suddenly recalled he was late for a very important date.

Mona rose from her desk and walked as quietly as she could to the office door. She opened it a few more inches and saw the man in the gallery, holding Tou-Tou and stroking his head.

"You have a black cat, Mona," he said. He wore the same three-piece suit as before. "How fitting."

"Tou-Tou's the gallery cat," she said. Cautiously she approached the man and took Tou-Tou from his arms. She wasn't sure she trusted him yet, and her cat was the closest thing Mona had to family. "Not much luck but he keeps me company."

"A cat to be envied then," the man said.

"Do you have a name?"

"Forgive me. I should have introduced myself last week. Malcolm."

"Malcolm," she repeated, liking the feel of it on her tongue. "Any last name?"

"Not at the moment. Was I correct about the painting?"

"You know you were. It was all over the news."

He shrugged a shoulder. "I pay very little attention to the news. A Reynolds, I assume?"

"It was. Appraised at five million."

"How much will you get?"

"Fifty-thousand-dollar finder's fee from the owner. Yours, of course."

"Why 'of course'?" he asked.

"I didn't even like the Morland. It was from his later years, after he stopped producing good work. I only displayed it because I thought it might sell for a couple thousand dollars. You're the one who told me there was something underneath it."

11

"What exactly was underneath it? Have you seen it?"

"The restorer says it appears to be a portrait of Nelly O'Brien. They've dubbed the painting *The Courtesan.* Reynolds even signed the canvas."

"Ahh, Miss O'Brien. Reynolds painted her several times, I believe."

"Once more than we'd realized. One art critic believes Morland painted over it during his debt years. Maybe he'd run out of canvases and couldn't afford more. He put a two-thousand-dollar painting over a five-million-dollar painting. The owner has decided to keep it in the family, but he's sending me the check this week."

"Put it toward saving your gallery," he said. "I have no interest in taking money from you. Quite the opposite, in fact."

"Thank you, Malcolm." She sat Tou-Tou down onto the floor. He didn't run back into the office as she expected him to. Instead, he lay on the floor between her and Malcolm as if he were as much a party to this conversation as they were. "That's very generous of you."

"I would like to be more generous with you."

"Why?" She couldn't keep the note of suspicion out of her tone.

"I have my reasons and they are very good reasons, but you wouldn't understand them, not yet. But eventually I will reveal all to you. *If* you agree to let me help you."

"Fifty thousand dollars is a good start," she said. "But I'm half a million in debt. I don't think anyone can help me."

"I've given you no reason to doubt me."

"What is it you want from me?"

"May I be blunt with you?" he asked.

"I'd prefer it."

"I very much wish to fuck you."

She opened her mouth and said nothing.

"Too blunt?" he asked, a slight smile on his lips.

"No, no." Mona waved her hand dismissively. "I appreciate the honesty. It's refreshing. I'm not sure how fucking me can help the gallery, but I thank you kindly for the offer."

"You must let me finish. But first, may we adjourn to your office? I prefer to discuss business in offices. That's what they're made for and they get a little jealous when they're neglected."

"Of course. This way."

She told herself that if he wanted to rape her and kill her, he could have done it by now and done it easily. He'd already proven he could slip in and out of the gallery without her knowledge even when the front door was locked. He was very tall—six foot or a little more by her reckoning, which was half a foot taller than she. Yet he hadn't so much as touched her. Not even a handshake. And Tou-Tou seemed to like him, not that she'd ever heard of a cat being a good judge of character.

Inside her office, she switched on the little Tiffany-style desk lamp and sat behind her desk. It was a small desk, feminine, with filigrees, and the chair was petite as well. But the chair across from her desk was made for a man of Malcolm's dimensions. A leather club chair, it fit him like a glove. He seemed the sort of man one would find in an old English club, no women allowed, old boys with money and power discussing politics behind the scenes. She wondered if he smoked cigars. She could smell the slightest trace of cigar smoke on his clothes. It was a masculine scent and not unpleasant in small doses.

"Business?" she asked.

"You're a very beautiful young lady," Malcolm said. "I like very beautiful young ladies."

"Do you?"

"I'm a connoisseur."

"Are you? Do you have a favorite type?"

"Elegant prostitutes," he said. "A perennial favorite."

"You know I'm not a prostitute, yes?" she asked.

"Not yet. But I think you'll make a fine whore."

She flinched at the word although he didn't say it like an insult. It sounded rather nice coming from him. Like a pet name almost.

"You enjoy using women for their bodies," she said.

"Yes, very much so."

"Most women prefer to be used for their minds."

"Foolishness," he said.

"Foolishness?"

"The mind is seated in the brain, yes?"

"Well…yes."

"The brain is an organ of the body. Whether I use you for your mind or use you for your cunt, I'm still using you for an organ of your body."

"You make an interesting point." The brain was indeed a bodily organ as were the genitals. She could hardly argue his logic.

"You're sitting on a goldmine, Mona. Literally."

She blushed. "I've never had my vagina called a goldmine before."

"Perhaps I was referring to your arse."

"Oh yes, hadn't thought of that."

"Why do I want to be generous with you, you asked me earlier. The answer is simple: I want to. Reason enough for me. If you want more to specifics, well, you're a beauty, as I said. Magnificent legs, marvelous ankles. And I love a girl with red hair, even if it is artificial. Your complexion is lighter than I prefer but it will show bites and blushes well. You wear your hair tastefully. Most women these days wear their hair shorn off or unbound and undone. Takes the magic out of the hair if it's already down and loose before we've gone to bed. You wear yours pinned up and it makes me imagine what it looks like down. I like that very much."

She warmed at the compliments.

"You could have seduced me for free, you know." If he had no qualms about admitting his attraction to her, she'd have none about admitting hers to him. "You are very handsome."

"Am I?"

"I like…" He'd enumerated her best features in detail. Surely he expected the same from her, yet she shied away from telling him how attractive she found him. He didn't seem the sort to need his ego massaged. "I like your hands."

"My hands."

"They're big," she said. "And muscular. Sort of. They have lovely veins in them. I like male hands with veins. I noticed them the first time I saw you. And surely you noticed me noticing them if you're such a connoisseur of women."

"I did."

"And yet you want to pay me for sex instead of simply asking me out on a date and getting it for free."

"Let me explain, darling." He leaned forward and rested an elbow on the chair arm. He used the hand attached to that arm and elbow to gesticulate as he spoke. "When a woman such as yourself and a man such as myself are lovers…" He pointed at her and then at himself. "Expectations are raised. Marriage being one of them. Lovers often love each other. I have no interest in love or marriage from you. Nor do I wish to take you to dinner. I simply want to fuck you in various ways that please me. It's my preference."

The phrase "in various ways" brought images into Mona's mind. She warmed even more. She started to cross her legs but caught herself in time.

"I have heard that men don't pay prostitutes for the sex itself. They pay prostitutes to leave."

He laughed softly, a warm sensual laugh. Now she did cross her legs.

"There may be some truth to that," Malcolm said. "A man can get the same thing from his wife as he could get from a whore, but the wife might want to talk after."

"God forbid."

"Indeed. I wouldn't pay you to leave, however. I'll do the leaving after. What I'm paying for, in fact, is permission. Carte blanche, shall we say."

"Carte blanche? Meaning?"

"I want your permission to do whatever I want to do with your body."

"Whatever you want? That doesn't sound safe."

"I realize that," he said. "I'll make you this promise—I won't damage you in any way. Will there be bites? Of course. Bruises? Undoubtedly. One can hardly kiss a girl as pale as you without leaving a mark. Will I make you bleed? Probably not, but it's happened before. I won't pull out your finger-nails or submit you to water torture. If you genuinely thought I wanted to do you real harm, I wouldn't be in this office negotiating with you, would I?"

"No."

"On the other hand, it's a virtual certainty I'll chain you to the bed and bugger you. I'm sure it will come as no shock to you that I am also very fond of riding crops."

"Riding crops?"

"Riding crops. They make the most delightful sound on naked female flesh. Ever heard it?"

"I haven't."

"You will."

"You think I'll agree to this?"

"I think you will." He sat back in the club chair again, steepled his fingers and looked at her over the top. "You're twenty-five years old, yes?"

"I am."

"A good age."

"And why is that?"

"Twenty-five means you're old enough to know better, young enough to do it anyway. Aren't you?"

"I'll admit I'm tempted. What are the terms?"

"In exchange for having carte blanche over your body—all three holes, thank you—I'll save The Red."

"You'll save my gallery." She ignored the comment about the holes. At least she tried to. Her body didn't ignore it nearly as well as she would have liked.

"I will," he said. "I can and I will."

"What's The Red to you?"

He raised his hands, palms up. "What can I say? I'm an art lover."

She believed there was more to it than that, but she didn't press him. The art world could be very shady—she knew that for a fact. Her mother had more than once allowed a painting with dubious provenance to be sold through the gallery. That was where Mona and her mother parted ways. Her mother loved the art world. Mona loved the art alone. But she'd also loved her mother, so she considered Malcolm's offer very seriously.

Mona leaned forward, put her elbows on her desk, clasped her hands in a prayer position.

"Half a million dollars," she said. "That's what I need just to get The Red out of the red."

"How long can you keep the gallery open with your finances in their current state?"

"One year at the most."

"How much do you need to stay open for five years?"

"Another half a million," she said, throwing out a grand sum.

"Are you making me an offer?" he asked.

"You are seriously willing to pay me that much money just to fuck me?"

He smiled at her. His dark eyes glinted like struck flint.

"You smile like the devil," Mona said.

"The devil doesn't smile," he said. "The devil smirks."

"You speak as if you know him."

"Would it shock you if I said I did?"

"It might be the least shocking thing you've said to me tonight. One million dollars simply to fuck me? Really? That's absurd."

"I'm not paying you a million dollars just to fuck you. Fucking you is the least of what I'll do to you. What I'm paying a million dollars for—minimum, mind you—is to fuck with you. Pardon my French."

She pardoned his French. She pardoned nothing else of his, however.

"It scares me to think what you'll expect from me for that amount of money. I'd rather sell myself for one hundred dollars than one million."

"You shouldn't let a man shake your hand for less than a hundred dollars, Mona. And you shouldn't be afraid."

"You won't do anything perverse to me?"

"I'll do everything perverse to you. But you still shouldn't be afraid."

"You threatened to fuck with me. What does that even mean?"

"We'll play games, you and I. Or I'll play them and you'll play along. You won't know reality from fantasy."

"I'll know."

"You say that now…but I'm very good at the games I play." This time he didn't smile. He smirked like she'd heard the devil does.

"How often would you expect to fuck with me? Every week? Every night?"

"Nothing like that. I'll expect no more than one night every one or two months."

"That's all?"

"I have…obligations elsewhere, let's say. I am a man enchained."

Married then? Sounded like it to her. Married or he had a girlfriend. Well, his other life was his business, not hers.

"How will you pay me? In cash? Check? We take cards at the gallery." While cash would be ideal, she'd love to see a check to find out who he was and where he lived.

"I'll pay you in the currency of the gallery. I'll pay you in art."

"You will pay me in art? You're a collector?"

"I am. And my private collection has been hidden away far too long. I can't think of a better way of bringing it to light again."

"You'll have to provide provenance. And considering I don't even know your last name…"

"I'll provide provenance at the end of the year. I'll give you the artwork after each night and you can have it authenticated and insured. When our year together is up, I'll provide impeccable provenance for all the pieces, which will increase their value and make it very easy for you to sell them."

"Impeccable, you say?"

"Impeccable and unimpeachable."

"Where will these assignations take place?"

"Your back room should do nicely for a playroom. The bed is back there, isn't it? The antique brass bed?"

She narrowed her eyes at him. "You know about the bed in the back?"

"I've seen the back room. It's where your mother kept the best pieces."

"The erotic pieces, you mean."

"Like I said, the best pieces."

"My mother was quite shameless. I'm not surprised you knew her."

"I am very sorry for the loss of your mother. Ophelia St. James was much beloved in the art community."

"She was. And this gallery was her life. She told me to do anything to save it."

"I can be anything," he said with the slightest smile.

"Yes," she said. "I imagine you could."

"Do we have an agreement then?" he asked.

"I have to think about this some more," she said. She turned in her chair to the side, rested her forehead on her hand and breathed.

"Do you have a lover?" he asked. "I won't tell you to stop seeing him if you do."

"We broke up," she said. "After Mother died."

"My condolences."

"No need for that. We were never in love, only lovers. He was a boy."

"Scandalous." Malcolm sounded far more pleased than scandalized.

"Not quite. I was twenty-four. He was eighteen. He lived in the apartment across from my mother's with his parents. In the last months I stayed with her every night, slept in the guest room. It was lonely sleeping there with my mother slowly dying in the next room." She shouldn't be telling Malcolm any of this and didn't know why she was, only that he seemed interested and it had been a very long time since she'd had a conversation this intimate with anyone.

"I certainly would have seduced the nearest available person as well," Malcolm said. "Even if my mother hadn't been dying."

"I can imagine that."

"You're welcome to imagine me seducing someone. I recommend it."

"Sadly, it wasn't much of a seduction," she said. "He was young and pretty and, best of all, lived five feet away. We would talk in the hallway when we met there. One night a neighbor came out of their apartment and shushed us for laughing, so I invited him in to finish the conversation. Mother was already asleep. Her pills knocked her out around nine every night. I didn't intend to go to bed with him, but the bed was the only place in the guest room to sit." She smiled at the memory of taking Ryan's virginity on the antique brass bed. She'd had to hold onto the headboard to keep it from rattling against the wall.

"You had every reason to, every right to," Malcolm said. "Anyone going through what you were would need the comfort of another body in your bed. Do you miss him?"

She shrugged. "I miss that time. I still had Mother by day and a lover by night. It was a precious few months for me. After she died, I sold the apartment to pay off some of the medical bills. I kept the brass bed. Mother had bought it years ago at an estate sale. She said it had once belonged to a courtesan so she couldn't resist buying it. She would buy anything if the origin story were good enough."

"It's a lovely bed. I'm certain it misses you. You should spend more time in it, with me preferably."

She missed the bed as well. Although her affair with Ryan had been brief, only three months, it had been a delicious distraction. They were lovers for the summer and knew the end date of their affair when they started—September, when Ryan would start college. He'd been a virgin, a tabula rasa, and she'd taught him exactly how to please her…and please her he did, two and sometimes three times a night. He'd slip in around ten, joining her in the antique brass bed where she lay waiting for him, already naked. They'd make love for two hours or more before he returned to his apartment down the hall. They spoke of nothing to each other but the sex. It was all they'd had in common. Yet, she missed him, or more accurately missed it—the sex, falling asleep with damp thighs, waking up with tender lips, tender nipples, having a secret reason to smile when no one else was looking. Malcolm offered all that to her, plus the money to save the gallery. How could she refuse? And yet…

"Condoms?" Mona asked. She hadn't used them with Ryan, but Ryan had been eighteen and a virgin.

"No," he said simply.

She had guessed as much. No one paid a million dollars to fuck someone and then put a layer of latex between their bodies.

"But you needn't worry," he said. "I won't give you any diseases."

"That's a comfort. Only one night every month or two?"

"That's all," he said. "But I assure you, they will be very long nights for both of us."

"Ten nights is a hundred thousand dollars a fuck. You do realize that you're overpaying me, yes?"

"I know it seems a bit, dear, but I will fuck you more than once a night. You'll earn it, I promise. If you're anything like the other Monas I've known, I have no doubt I'll get my money's worth and then some."

Twelve months. A handful of nights. Four or five times a night, if not more. And all for one million dollars.

"If any of this art of yours is stolen—"

"I'm a whoremonger, a rake, and a degenerate, my dear, but I am not a thief."

"Forgive me but I had to ask," she said. "Art theft is the fourth largest international crime behind guns, drugs, and human trafficking."

"Only fourth?" He sounded disgusted. He sighed, as if disappointed with the world. "No accounting for taste."

It was that joke that did it. Until then she'd been sitting on the fence, torn between needing the money and wanting her dignity. But when he gave a little roll of his eyes as if affronted that anyone would consider drugs or guns more worth stealing and selling than art…she fell off the fence and right into Malcolm's lap.

"One million dollars," she said. "You have carte blanche for one year. We'll meet here. Is that the agreement?"

"It is indeed. Are you saying yes?" he asked.

"The deal is done after one year? You won't expect anything else from me? Any favors, sexual or otherwise? A stake in the gallery? Counterfeit provenance?"

"Nothing of the sort. After our final encounter you won't even see me again. Ever."

Ever?

"Well…you've certainly proven your bona fides with the Reynolds painting," she said. "And I promised my mother I wouldn't sell The Red."

"Deathbed promises are the most serious," he said. "We must keep them at all costs."

"How did you know it was a deathbed promise?"

"An assumption. You see, I made one myself."

"To your mother?"

"No. If she said anything about me on her deathbed it was to curse my name. Luckily I was elsewhere at the time," he said and smiled. She had never understood the phrase "devastatingly handsome" before meeting Malcolm, but when he left this room, she would feel devastated to be in his presence no longer. It all made sense.

"My mother loved this gallery," she said. "It was her life. Now that she's gone, it may be the death of me."

"I won't allow that, Mona." He seemed to find her name amusing.

"I have a feeling I'll regret this…"

"I have a feeling you won't."

"You would say that."

"I would," he readily admitted. "But you'll say it too in a year. I assume you'll accept the fifty-thousand-dollar finder's fee from the Reynolds as a down payment?"

"I think that's reasonable," she said.

"Then we're in agreement?"

What did she have to lose? Other than her health, her sanity, her spotless criminal record, her business, and her life?

"We're in agreement," she said.

He clapped his hands, rubbed them together, and stood up.

"Excellent. Just what I've been wanting to hear for a very long time. We'll start tomorrow night."

"So soon?"

"Does your cunt have a prior engagement?" he asked, his tone mocking.

"Tomorrow night, then. Is there…" She paused, not sure what she was asking. "Are there rules? Expectations of me? Requests?"

He held up one finger, telling her to sit and wait. She sat. She waited. He walked to her bookshelf and perused the titles, the hand on his chin again like the first night. At last he seemed to find what he was looking for. He pulled a large white book from the shelf and leafed through the pages. Then he returned to her desk, bringing the book with him.

"That," he said, laying the book open on the desk and pointing at a photograph of a painting. "I would like you to wait for me thusly."

The painting in the photograph was one she knew well—

Manet's *Olympia*, a portrait of a young girl, naked, lying on a bed with her head up and staring directly at the viewer. It was an infamous painting, Manet making mockery of the tired old Venus-reclining-on-her-bed trope. Olympia was a prostitute and a shameless one at that. When it was first displayed, the crowds found it so vulgar they wanted to tear it to shreds.

"So I'm to be your Olympia."

"For what I'm paying you, you'll be everything I want you to be."

She looked up at him, met his eyes. For the first time since they met, he touched her. He laid his hand on the side of her face, stroked the arch of her cheekbone with his thumb. Such a large warm hand. She truly believed she would regret making this agreement. But she didn't regret it now.

"You were meant to do this," he said softly. "You'll see."

"Why me?" she asked. "Millions of women in this country, millions in yours…why me?"

"Millions of paintings in this world. Only one Mona Lisa. Billions of women in this world. Only one you, Mona Lisa St. James."

Then he left her in the office, blushing and shivering and undeniably aroused. She'd just agreed to become a prostitute to save her gallery.

Something told Mona that somewhere out there, her mother was proud of her.

III: OLYMPIA

*M*alcolm had picked a good day for a tryst. Sunday was the gallery's shortest day—open only from one to five. After she closed The Red, Mona went shopping. She didn't need much—a velvet choker, a flower for her hair, clean white sheets for the bed, all easy to find. At her apartment she showered and shaved and waxed until she was as smooth as a marble statue. Malcolm hadn't told her to remove her hair, but Olympia had no visible body hair in Manet's painting. Mona should have asked him what he preferred. She knew he would have told her had she asked. A shameless man, he'd made her feel rather shameless. In fact, the whole conversation with Malcolm had been rather digni-fied. She hadn't felt embarrassed or ashamed. It felt like a business transaction, which she had appreciated.

After all, she was a businesswoman.

She was glad Malcolm had given her instructions for what to wear and how to wait for him. It made it easier. No second-guessing. Before dressing to leave her apartment, she stood in front of her full-length mirror and examined her naked body. She wasn't thin exactly, certainly not skinny. She had breasts larger than her frame but no man had ever complained about that. Her legs were her best feature, if she did say so herself. The face? A straight nose, full lips, high cheekbones, high forehead, which is why she wore blunt bangs. The verdict? She'd make a passable Olympia and a very fine whore indeed. She was getting used to that word. In fact, she was starting to like it. It gave her a thrill to think of herself that way. A goldmine, that's what Malcolm had called her body. A goldmine. Who wouldn't go digging if one were sitting on a goldmine? Only a fool.

She could only hope she wasn't fooling herself.

Mona dressed in a long breezy skirt, sandals, a white bra, white panties, and white cotton top. Her usual casual summer uniform. The streets were humid when she walked to the gallery four blocks away and by the time she unlocked the door, she was sweating. It was a relief to step into the air-conditioning. In her office, she caught Tou-Tou sleeping in the leather club chair Malcolm had sat in.

"You know better than that," she said to Tou-Tou, as she scooped him up and set him on the floor. "Company only. You have your own bed."

He looked at her, affronted, as if to say "How dare you judge me? I know what you're doing here…"

Or perhaps she was merely being paranoid. Tou-Tou followed at her heels as she went into the back storage room. She switched on the floor lamp, as the room was windowless but for the single skylight above the bed. This had always been her favorite part of the gallery. It was full of odd and gorgeous clutter. Here were the strange paintings her mother had loved but could never unload. Erotic paintings mostly. A woman in a red dress with one strap dangling off her shoulder, a bare breast exposed. A naked couple fornicating on a boat while the ship sank and sailors drowned. A lady in Victorian garb whipping the corpulent ass of a naked man with a branch of holly. All good company for such a liaison as Mona's tonight.

She wondered if the paintings would give Malcolm any ideas.

In addition to the paintings, antique furniture was scattered here and there—a red velvet fainting couch, a cheval mirror with an ornately carved frame hidden under a white sheet, a Rococo-style chair with carved wood arms and red and gold striped fabric. They were for parties, special events. When she was a little girl, Mona would come here after school and nap on the fainting couch, dance in front of the mirror, sit in the Rococo chair and read her little school books, while her mother in the other room hobnobbed with artists, art critics, art lovers, and anyone else who wanted to come in from the rain.

And, of course, there was the brass bed. It had been her bed as a girl growing up in her mother's apartment. She'd lost her virginity in that bed and taken Ryan's in it as well. Her memories of that bed, in that bed, were potent ones. After tonight it would hold even more memories.

She prayed they would be good ones.

Funny, the last night she'd slept in this bed was the night her mother died, the night her mother had made her promise to keep the gallery, no matter what. And now she'd keep her promise in that bed. She only hoped her mother would understand. Mona looked over her shoulder at the portrait of a handsome, randy old duke naked from the waist down with his penis poking inside the squirming girl on his lap.

Oh yes, her mother would very likely understand.

And approve.

Mona had stripped the bed of sheets and blankets when it was brought to the storage room. They'd been old flannel sheets, pilling and faded. If she were going to whore herself, she would do it on high thread count Egyptian cotton. In

Manet's *Olympia* painting, the sheets on the bed were white, as was the coverlet. She'd found an old white quilt in her mother's things and put that on the bed. When she finished, the bed looked lush and inviting. The temptation to lay in the bed was strong, lay in it and touch herself. Should she prime her body a little bit before Malcolm arrived? Would he want her to be wet when she greeted him?

Well, it's not likely he'd be displeased if she was.

She stripped naked and put her clothes on the seat of the wooden chair she'd placed at the end of the bed. Olympia wore a flower in her hair, so Mona tucked one into her side bun. She tied the red velvet choker around her neck. Finally, she adjusted the lamp so that a gentle golden halo of light surrounded the bed and left the rest of the room in shadows. Then she lay down to wait.

Though the sheets screamed luxury, decadence, and comfort, she could not relax. It was eleven now. Malcolm would likely arrive at midnight as he had the past two times he'd visited the gallery. She felt so awkward lying there naked. This wasn't her. Not at all. No matter what Malcolm said, this wasn't her. But for the sake of the gallery she would try anyway. She imagined herself lying stiff and unmoving underneath Malcolm as his cock jabbed at her tight, dry vagina. That wouldn't do. It would be agony. He'd tear her and she'd bleed all over the white sheets. She wished she'd thought to bring wine and drink a glass or two. Instead she'd only brought a few bottles of water, a bowl of cut strawberries, and apples.

Closing her eyes, Mona breathed deeply into her body, pulling the breaths into her lungs and belly. She imagined the real Olympia. She must have existed, or a girl much like her. The painting had shocked viewers for the forthright way Olympia held up her head. Shameless, she was. Unapologetic. Why should she apologize? It was the men who paid her for sex. She was merely doing what she'd been told to do all her life: submit her body and will to men. How dare those men judge her? They'd created her. A woman can't sell her body without clients to buy it. Olympia would laugh all the way to the bank and then likely spread her legs for the bank president in exchange for free checking.

What a girl.

Mona smiled. She wished she'd had Olympia's courage. She wouldn't be shaking on the bed while waiting for her next customer. No, she would bathe herself—a whore's bath, washing the leavings of her previous client out of her. She'd repair her coiffure. It must be just right. She'd dab perfume between her thighs, behind her ears, between her breasts. She'd drink white wine to wash the taste of the last man from her mouth. She would recline on her bed and massage her breasts to bring her nipples to hardness so that when her next client came into the room, he would think she was aroused at the very sight of him.

She heard the door opening.

Mona lifted her head. Malcolm stood in the doorway in his three-piece suit.

"Ahh..." he breathed. "My Olympia."

Mona didn't know what to say, so she said nothing. Malcolm didn't seem to mind her silence. He came to the bed and sat beside her. She sat propped up on her pillow and frozen on the sheets, shivering.

"You look so lovely," he said softly, his gaze grazing her naked body from face to feet and up again. "I'll enjoy you tonight."

"I'm nervous," she said.

"Of course you are. I wouldn't want or expect anything else."

"You want me to be nervous?"

"Very much. It will make the triumph all the sweeter. I

love the challenge of overcoming reluctance." He bent and kissed her chest over her racing heart. Then he stood and walked to the end of the bed where he proceeded to undress. First the suit jacket came off, then the vest. He unfastened his buttons with agile fingers. He didn't make a production of undressing, and yet she couldn't take her eyes off him as he peeled out of his shirt to reveal strong sculpted biceps, a flat hard stomach, and a broad chest. The shoes were next and then the trousers. Her eyes widened at the first glimpse of his cock, already erect and glistening at the tip. She watched it as he walked back to her, taking in its impressive size and even more impressive girth. She would need to be very wet to enjoy that inside of her.

"You're pleased with me?" he asked and she sensed the question wasn't a question at all. A statement of fact. He knew she was. He simply wanted her to admit it.

"I am. Although…"

"I'll take care of everything," he said. "I haven't lost a woman to it yet."

She laughed and it helped ease her fears. He sat on the bed again at her side. He touched the side of her face, caressed her cheekbone, pushed her bangs to the side and kissed her forehead.

"I'm so pleased you've agreed to this," he said. "Very pleased. It's been a long time."

"For me too."

"Then we'll both enjoy this."

"Although it's for you, isn't it?" she asked.

"What do you mean?"

"I mean, you're paying for me. You can do what you want. It doesn't matter if I enjoy it or not."

"I do hope you'll enjoy it," he said. "But it's not a require-ment. In general, however, your pleasure gives me pleasure. Not everything I do will be physically pleasurable for you, however. For me, yes, but not for you. That was the nature of our agreement, yes?"

"Yes," she said, nodding.

"There's still time to change your mind. I don't force women. It would be beneath even such a man as myself."

She shook her head. "I want to do it."

"Even if you don't enjoy the sex—and you will—you'll certainly enjoy the money."

"I plan to," she said. Not the money itself, but the freedom money would buy her.

He smiled his devil's grin, but didn't look as devilish as the first night. He was only a man after all. A handsome man, naked, and lovely to behold.

"Good. Very good. Now spread your legs for me. Very wide."

She pulled her knees up, sliding her feet along the sheets and then letting her legs fall open. Malcolm looked at her without touching, merely examining the goods he'd bought.

"You didn't have to remove your hair," he said. "Prostitutes shaved in the old days to remove lice. Luckily you don't seem to have that problem."

"I thought perhaps she was so young she didn't have pubic hair yet. Perhaps that was why the painting was so scandalous."

"The art world didn't care about young women selling their bodies. They only cared if someone dared to break their rules of composition, of acceptable subject matter. You could show a naked woman hiding her face or lying supine and limp as a wet rag. God forbid he paint a girl who dared them to look her in the eyes."

"They were fools," she said.

"They were scared," he countered. "A woman with power. A woman who owned her body and wasn't afraid to sell it. That painting is art because it terrified its first viewers. Art should be dangerous, you know. It should say something to society that society doesn't want to hear. Do you know what the opposite of art is? Propaganda. There's too much of that in the world. Not enough art. And certainly not enough of this..."

Malcolm dipped his head and pressed a kiss on her pubis over her clitoris. He exhaled warm air over her sensitive bare flesh and she shivered. He lifted his head but only to open her labia with his fingers. He wasn't gentle when he touched her, but not rough either. Perfunctory. Businesslike.

"Perfect," he said when he had her spread out for him. "A work of art." He dipped his head again and licked the hole he'd uncovered, even pushing his tongue against and into it. It wasn't exactly pleasurable but she found no reason to object. It felt so odd to be used in this manner. No dinner first. No tender kisses. No foreplay other than a discussion of art history, which, for a woman like her, was arousing in its own way.

His tongue sought and found her clitoris as he stretched out on the bed to give his full attention to arousing her. Her clitoris started to awaken as he lapped at it with long slow motions of his tongue. He circled it, sucked it lightly, and circled it again. The first quiet gasp of pleasure escaped Mona's lips. Malcolm said nothing about it but she sensed it pleased him. He'd paused when she'd done it and then licked her again in the same way that had pulled the sigh from her lips. With his fingertips he spread her open again and licked her inner labia, her folds, and the entrance of her body again. She wanted to touch his hair or his shoulders but wasn't sure if that was allowed. She gripped the sheets in her fingers instead.

"Delicious," Malcolm murmured and she felt the word as hot puffs of air against her clitoris. His tongue swirled around it again, making it swell, making it ache. She felt it throbbing against his lips. Then he touched it with his fingertips, putting pressure on it right where she needed it. His touch wasn't rough, but insistent, and the throbbing grew harder. It throbbed like a pulse point, pumping blood through her hips.

Again he turned his tongue on her, those long deep strokes right across and around the core of her pleasure. All sensation was concentrated in that tiny throbbing little organ. Every nerve was alive there, every muscle poised for release. She was so wet now—dripping—he could have put his cock into her with one brutal thrust and she could have and would have taken it all. He didn't penetrate her then, although in the haze of her arousal she could have sworn she'd begged him to.

She'd go mad if he didn't let her come. She was already wild with the need for it, squirming under his mouth, pumping her hips, grasping at the sheets to give her leverage. She pushed against his mouth, needing more and more and more. The muscles inside of her clenched and released, clenched again tighter. Her vaginal walls were slick and ready. She was ready. She had never been more ready.

When she could bear no more, and a scream rested on the tip of her tongue, Malcolm abruptly rose up and mounted her. With his hands on her hips, he impaled her with a deep hard stroke. She came with a cry, arching and writhing, as he thrust wildly into her. In the midst of her orgasm he came into her, ejaculating deep into her. She felt it pouring out of her even as his hips kept pumping, dragging her climax and his out as long as he could. It felt endless. The contractions were so sharp they almost hurt. She felt one muscle in partic-ular, a tight little muscle near her cervix, fluttering wildly as Malcolm filled her with his thick semen.

She was getting paid for this.

Finally, it was over. Malcolm put his hands on either side

of her body and dropped his head while her vagina gave its little final gasps. She lifted her head and looked between her legs, at the large organ splitting her open. She waited for him to pull out of her. He didn't.

Slowly he began to thrust again. She couldn't quite believe it. She kept watching as he withdrew from her pussy and slid inside again. It seemed impossible she could take so much but she saw it with her own eyes—thick inch after thick inch disappearing inside her and reappearing slicked with her wetness and his. Surely he couldn't mean to fuck her again so soon. She wasn't ready, but that didn't matter to him, did it? This was the arrangement.

Mona looked up at his face while he fucked her. His eyes were closed and he seemed to be utterly lost in the pleasure of his thrusting. His lips were slightly parted and she wanted to touch them, but didn't. He was using her, using her body, using her hole. She didn't move with him, merely lay underneath and watched his thigh muscles flex and release with his thrusts. It didn't hurt. She was dripping wet and her body offered no resistance at all. He'd tunneled into her, opened her up, and made himself at home inside her. It felt vaguely pornographic, lying there on the bed, watching him fuck her. It could have been any woman on his cock but it so happened to be her. The pumping of his hips was mesmerizing. How long could he go on? She looked forward to finding out. His breathing was heavy, not labored, but his entire body had gone tense again. He had the sheets in a death grip. The veins in his hands she found so attractive didn't end at his wrists but snaked up his arms all the way to the biceps.

"Who are you…" she breathed.

Malcolm's eyes fluttered open and he looked down at her. "You'll find out," he said.

"When? Where?"

"Eventually. In this bed. Any other questions?"

"May I touch you?"

"You may. Always, unless told otherwise."

She raised her hands to his shoulders. They were iron under her palms. Such a hard man—hard body, hard cock, hard to read, hard to believe he was real even as he pounded into her very convincing proof of his existence.

"Open wider," he said and she spread her legs even more for him. She'd never spread this wide before because no lover had ever told her to. Inside she felt her muscles shifting, moving, finding new ways to accommodate the large organ penetrating her. He reached between their joined bodies and wetted his fingertips with their fluids. He massaged the wetness into her clitoris and it swelled instantly at his touch. It would burst if he didn't stop. She would burst. Her pussy split open wide, the thrumming and throbbing, it was all happening again. A low moan built in the back of her throat. Malcolm rammed her with quick, deep thrusts. She had to hold the headboard to steady herself. The orgasm hit her with blinding force. It was obliterating. Her shoulders rose off the bed while her sex spasmed all around the organ inside her, trying to grip it and hold it in place because at that moment her body wanted him in it more than it had ever wanted anything before in her life. She wanted it, needed it, and if he ever took it out of her she would wither up and die.

Mona collapsed back onto the bed again, sweating and panting. Very slowly, very carefully, Malcolm eased out of her. She winced as he pulled out, tender as she was from his merciless thrusts. She'd never been fucked quite that hard. Then again, no man had ever paid for the privilege of fucking her quite that hard so she couldn't blame him for wanting to get his money's worth.

Malcolm lay on his side next to her, propped up on his elbow.

"See?" he said. "You make a marvelous whore."

"You say that like it's a compliment." She talked in a rasping whisper. He'd stolen her breath away.

"It is. It most certainly is a compliment."

"You didn't come again?"

His erection pressed against her bare thigh, brutally hard still.

"I wanted to linger in your cunt awhile. I found it quite welcoming."

"Make yourself at home," she sighed.

"I intend to."

She smiled wanly. She could fall asleep right now and not wake up for ten straight hours. That's how much the sex had taken out of her. Her legs were still open wide because she hadn't the energy to close them. Semen dripped out of her onto the sheets. It itched and tickled all at the same time. She felt debauched but not debased. She wasn't sure what the difference was, but there was one, she knew it.

"Lovely, lovely hole," he said as he put his hand between her legs and stroked her wet inner lips before slipping two fingers inside of her. He poked and prodded around, seeking soft spots and tender spots, sensitive spots that exulted in being touched. "Quite tight. Very hot inside, very wet. Strong muscles. I thought you wouldn't let me out of there for a moment."

"I didn't want to. Right before I came I felt like I'd die if you ever took your cock out of me."

"You're not the first girl who's told me that. I know how to choose my women well." He smiled. She was starting to like the smile very much. "I likely won't allow you to climax unless I'm inside you. I prefer it that way."

Had he been a boyfriend she might have raised an objection. She loved coming from oral alone and often had. Malcolm had taken her to the very edge of orgasm with his tongue but then he'd penetrated her at the last moment.

"If you prefer it that way…" Her voice trailed off.

"Your pleasure is for my pleasure," he reminded her. "When you come on my cock, I feel it. That's all there is to it."

She smiled. "I won't complain."

"No, I don't think you will. You're too good of a whore for that."

"You do like your whores, don't you?" she asked.

"I have trouble respecting a woman who gives away for free what she could sell for good money. Whores are the only women who know their own worth. I mean that."

"What about male prostitutes?"

"Their clients are generally men as well. I don't fault anyone who takes a man to the bank before going to bed with him. I wouldn't let a strange man put his finger in my mouth and whores take far more into their bodies every single night. It's skilled, brave work. Bless those lasses, they've saved my life and damned my soul. What more could I ask for?"

"You're a strange man."

"And you…you are a beautiful whore." He bent his head and kissed her lips. He'd already fucked her twice—his semen was inside her, and his fingertip pressed gently against her cervix—and yet this was their very first kiss. It wasn't a gentle kiss, not tender, but sensual and warm. He tasted like an old Irish whisky, which she liked, and he knew how to use his tongue, which she loved. He kissed her from her lips to her neck. She murmured a pleased sigh when he took her breast in his hand and squeezed it lightly, then slightly harder.

"I was wondering when you were going to do that," she said.

"I haven't fucked in quite a while. Getting in your cunt was my top priority. But these lovely nipples are a close second. Very close."

He slid on top of her, straddling her at the waist. He pressed her wrists into the bed on either side of her head and held her down. First he licked her right nipple, then licked it again. He licked it like he'd licked her clitoris, long slow passes of his tongue. Her nipple hardened and as soon as it did he sucked it into his mouth. Mona turned her head and watched him suckling at her breast. He was intent on the task, his eyes closed, as he drew the nipple and aureole all the way into his mouth. It wasn't a comfortable sensation, this intense pulling. He sucked hard and for a long time. She had to remember he was doing this for himself. He'd paid for the privilege of doing what he wanted to her body. And something told her this was merely the tip of the iceberg.

Despite the discomfort, she found herself growing aroused again. Perhaps there was a part of her that responded to being used by a man for his pleasure. She certainly couldn't stop watching him sucking her nipple. He was latched on tight and he didn't seem ready to stop any time soon. Blood rushed to her breast. Inside his hot mouth he swirled his tongue around the peak. Her nipple felt hard as a diamond to her. He let it go but only to pinch it between thumb and forefinger, pinch it and pull it and tug it. He released one of her wrists to slap her breast. He struck it with his open hand, not terribly hard, but hard enough to sting, then slapped again a little harder. Another slap followed by a squeeze, more tugging and pulling of her nipple, a pinch, a pull, a tug, and another long, long suckling. She panted, moaned, her head swimming from the riot of sensation. Her breast felt swollen and heavy and so terribly tender.

Without warning he turned his attention to her left breast. He slapped it too, grabbed it and groped it roughly. She cried out when he pinched the nipple painfully hard but right afterward, he put his mouth on it and the sudden shift in sensation had her crying out in pleasure. He sucked the nipple deep into his mouth, sucked and kept sucking until she groaned loudly in the back of her throat. He released it, sat up and back onto her hips and slapped both her breasts with his hands, slapped and grabbed them, slapped and massaged them. Quick pain followed quickly by slow pleasure. She didn't know what to feel. She accustomed herself to one and then had to immediately get used to another. Was this what her previous lovers had wanted to do to her breasts? Handle them roughly, squeeze and slap them, suck and pull them? Were they all too polite, too well-trained? Is this the way men behaved behind the curtain of civility? Is this what all her lovers would have done had they bought her body with money instead of with charm and the empty promises of love someday, perhaps, maybe?

She rather thought she preferred it on this side of the curtain.

Her nipples were almost purple from how hard he'd suckled them. And her breasts were bright red and burning from the slaps of his hands. He held both breasts in his large hands, held them hard, hard enough to see all those veins she so enjoyed looking at. Pinned beneath him by his weight, she could barely move her hips, but she tried. She wanted him to feel her body begging for his cock.

"Not yet, darling," he said. "Not quite yet. I'm having far too much fun to stop now."

He rolled her breasts, molded them against his palms, lifted them and held them. There was nothing of the savage about him, but nothing of the gentleman either. He was simply a man behaving like a man.

She liked this man.

Abruptly he stopped and slid off her stomach.

"Come," he ordered, taking her by the arm and pulling her to her feet off the bed.

She felt like a mannequin as he moved her this way and that, turning her back to his chest, bending her over the bed, placing her hands just so on the covers, and then sticking his prick into her from behind without a word of warning. He held her hips while he pumped it into her, controlling the depth and the speed entirely. He gave. She took. This would be her role for the next year when they met. She was to take it, whatever it was. Sometimes she would enjoy what he gave her. Sometimes she would not. He had told her that already...but now she believed him. His penis was long and large and every few thrusts the tip would hit her cervix, something she found uncomfortable to say the least. But Malcolm was enjoying himself, fucking her like this. His every breath and grunt and groan told her he was. So she stayed loose-limbed in his grasp, her tender breasts swaying with his every rough deep thrust, and waited it out.

At last he came, shooting her full of his hot thick fluid. It slicked her thighs and the male scent of it permeated the room. The scent of sex. The scent of a man with his whore.

The scent of money.

Malcolm pulled out of her and patted her on the ass.

"Good lass," he said. "Well done."

"Thank you." She slowly stood up straight and took a deep breath.

"Take a moment," he said as he laid on the bed again. "You've earned a little rest."

She was desperately thirsty from panting so hard.

"Water?" she asked.

"Please."

She pulled the little basket she'd packed out from under the bed. From it she took out two green glass bottles of sparkling water.

"Dangerous," he said.

"What is?"

"Glass bottles."

"Why so?"

He smiled.

"You wouldn't," she said.

He cocked his head to the side, raised his eyebrow.

"All right," she said as she unscrewed the cap of the bottle. "You would."

"It isn't that I would. It is that I will. You do realize this is merely foreplay, don't you? We haven't even started yet. I like to play games. I like to play roles. I might even bring an audience one night or two. I might even bring friends…"

If this was nothing but foreplay, nothing but the opening act, what would the main attraction be like?

"You didn't bring the riding crop," she said.

"Not tonight. Would you like me to bring it for our next assignation?"

"I have a choice?" She handed him a bottle of water.

"You have a choice of when, not if. There is no if. I will beat you with a riding crop at some point in the next twelve months."

"Might as well," she said. She wasn't looking forward to being beaten with a crop, but it seemed it would be best to get it over with. Maybe she would like it. Only one way to find out.

"We'll see," he said. "Drink your water."

She drank her water deep and he sipped at his. His stamina was remarkable. He had the sexual energy of a teenage boy and the lasting power of a man. A potent combination.

"Is this something you do often?" she asked. She sat on the bed, cross-legged like a child in school.

"Fuck?"

"No. Find women in need and turn them into whores?"

"You aren't my first. You will be my last, however." He

gave her his half-drunk water bottle and she set it on the floor beside the bed. Then he laid back on the pillows, stretched out. His penis lay limp and draped on his thigh, a sleeping giant.

"Why is that?"

"I made a promise I fully intend to keep. With your assistance, of course."

"That's a very cryptic thing to say."

"I'm afraid I can't explain any better than that. I think you'll understand eventually."

"If I'm your last, I hope I'm also your best." She took a final drink of her water, finishing the bottle.

"I have no doubt you'll give me my money's worth," he said with a grin. Then he raised his hand and crooked his finger at her, beckoning her to him. She started to put her empty bottle on the floor and he shook his head. "Bring it here."

She froze, but only for a moment. He must have his money's worth.

"Lay on your back," he said. "Open up."

She did as he told her, opening her legs for him.

"Pleasure yourself with your fingers," he said. "Use both hands."

Her vulva still dripped with his semen and her labia were swollen and sensitive to the touch. With two fingers on each hand she caressed her folds as he watched, parting them, spreading them wide.

"Touch your clit," he said. "Pull back the hood."

She took a ragged breath. His eyes gleamed rapaciously as he watched her pull back the flesh to reveal the tiny knot of tissue underneath.

"Hold there," he said softly. "Don't move a single muscle."

He bent and with the tip of his tongue touched her exposed clitoris. A light touch, but it felt like a bolt of light-

43

ning shot through her from that point of contact to the base of her neck and the heels of her feet.

"Rub yourself the way you do when you're alone," he instructed. "Like you're trying to make yourself come, but don't."

She nodded and shifted her two fingers into a small V-shape, the pad of each finger on either side of her clitoris. Slowly, she made a circular motion, then an oval, pulling the hood lightly with each apex and nadir. As she did so, Malcolm picked up the water bottle and examined it. It wasn't a large bottle—only about six inches tall with a narrow neck and a round bulb of a base, a typical glass water bottle. There was no paper label on it, only paint. She'd taken off the screw cap. It was just glass, she told herself. Thick smooth glass and he was sliding it, mouth first, into the hole. She moaned as the cool glass pressed against her hot inner flesh. Smooth, so very smooth, but hard as well, unbearably hard. Thick at the base, too thick to take all the way in. And yet as she rubbed herself harder and faster, she wanted it in. Could she take it? Malcolm seemed in no hurry to force the matter. He pushed it in and then allowed her body to push it back out again. He pushed it in. Her body pushed it out. His dark eyes were trained on the sight; he looked only at her pussy and the bottle.

"I once poured wine, bottle and all, into a pretty whore's cunt and drank it out of her," he said in a low and faraway voice. "Evangeline. A freckled ginger. She was the bastard daughter of a duke."

"Did she like it?"

"She liked me. There wasn't anything she wouldn't let me do to her. One evening, I played cards with her father and beat him. I rolled up the money I won from him, slipped it in a bottle, and put the bottle in his daughter's cunt that very night. When I told her where I'd gotten the money, she laughed so hard the bottle shot out of her and shattered on the floor. Coins went everywhere. I nearly pissed myself. What a sight."

"You've had adventures, haven't you?"

"Haven't you?"

"Not until you," she said. "And probably not after you either."

"Oh, you'll have an adventure after I'm gone. I'll see to it."

"I bet you will," she said. Malcolm only smiled and forced the bottle in a little deeper. Her muscles stretched and opened to receive it. The longer she touched herself the more she wanted it. She felt a deep muscle contraction and it was so delicious she almost orgasmed right there.

"Be good," he said.

"Trying."

"This is a show," he said. "And you're putting it on for me. Entertain me, not yourself. Entertain me."

His tone was commanding and she responded well to that tone. She put her heels on the bed, flexed her hips, lifting them as she pulled in her stomach muscles to turn her body concave so that he could see her pussy better. With both hands she pulled her labia apart as he pushed the bottle in so deep her vagina nearly engulfed it. It slid out of her, but Malcolm eased it back in as she once more pulled the labia apart. She could take it. She could. She knew she could if she could only open up a tiny bit more. Her body was so tense it almost hurt to shift her thighs a few inches wider. But she did and as Malcolm pressed the bottle in, the heel of his palm against the base, she inhaled and drew it into her all the way, entirely.

"Hold it in," Malcolm said. His hand covered her entire pubis, blocking the bottle's exit. She clutched at the sheets, her body taut, tense, and ready to snap. But she held it, she held her breath and held the bottle in her. Malcolm tapped the base of the bottle and she felt vibrations all through her hips. She groaned, moaned like the whore he'd made her. More taps, more vibrations. He put two fingers on the base of the glass and moved it side to side, up and down, around in a circle. The pleasure was maddening. She'd never taken so much. She had never been opened up and filled like this. Not even his huge organ had split her so wide as this. She came up on her elbows, unable to believe it was happening, but when looked between her thighs, there it all was—the bottle buried in her, Malcolm's hand holding it in, her clitoris swollen more than it had ever been before. She pushed air through her lips like a woman giving birth.

"What do you want?" Malcolm asked. "Do you want it in or out?"

"I don't know," she breathed.

"I like it in. Very nice," he said. "But you must be about to die, aren't you? Wouldn't you love to come?"

"I need to."

"You don't need to. You want to. And I want to keeping fucking you with the bottle. Push it out."

"This is…perverse," she said between breaths.

"Don't complain," he said. "I could have used a wine bottle."

She tightened her inner muscles and forced it out of her. She watched it emerge from her wet sex and into Malcolm's hand. But as soon as it was out to the mouth of the bottle, Malcolm eased it back into her, all the way in again. He slid his arm under her shoulders and she lay back across it. The position forced her back to bend and thrust her breasts into the air. Malcolm licked and sucked at her nipple as he toyed with the bottle inside her. Mona begged him to let her orgasm, implored him, offered up her body to him, which was meaningless since he'd already bought it from her.

"Soon…" was all he said. Soon. He rasped it into her ear.

Her body shook and shivered, shook and tensed. She had to come, had to, absolutely must...

He was fully erect again, his cock pressed against her thigh. She reached down and grasped it in her hand, held it simply to hold it, this instrument of her pleasure and her torment. Malcolm shuddered and chuckled, no doubt amused by her desperation. The begging went on. Soon the only word she knew was "please." She said it over and over. Finally, he gave in.

"Push it out," he said and she rolled up again to force the bottle out of her. Malcolm mounted her quickly, penetrating her with a stroke. With her breasts in his hands, he rode her into the bed. The thrusts were rough and rapid and bruising. He squeezed her breasts with brutal strength, and she didn't care, not at all. She cared only about the huge hard shaft slamming into her over and over. She arched into the orgasm, crying out louder than she ever had, her vagina closing in quick contractions all around the brutal organ inside her. Her entire body flinched with the muscle spasms. God, what was he doing to her? How could she ever return to a normal life after this?

She collapsed back onto the pillows and Malcolm pulled out of her. She rolled onto her side and he lay beside her, his chest to her back.

"I have to sleep," she said as he kissed the side of her neck under her ear. "I can't go on anymore. I have to sleep...just for a minute. I think you killed me..."

She was out of her mind with exhaustion. Malcolm laughed that gentle mocking laugh again. He pulled the red rose from behind her ear, unpinned her hair and let it lay free on the pillow. He teased her nose with the petals and kissed the back of her neck.

"Sleep then," he said. "I don't mind. Sleep and I'll take you while you're sleeping."

"You wouldn't…"

"Don't you know better than that by now, darling?"

Mona did know better than that by now. Smiling, she nodded, shifted forward onto her stomach, her knee up to leave her sex open to him. As she drifted off to sleep, she felt him enter her again. Surely she couldn't sleep with his cock inside her. But the thrusts were long and slow and for once, quite gentle. They were steady and rhythmic and it was as if he was rocking her to sleep. And she fell asleep with him inside her, his warm breath on her naked shoulder, her name on his lips as he kissed her earlobe.

When she woke, sunlight streamed through the skylight over the bed and Malcolm was gone. Slowly she rolled up and pressed a hand to her forehead. The last thing she remembered was Malcolm taking the red rose from her hair and the velvet choker off her neck and penetrating her gently from behind.

If asked, she doubted she'd swear on a Bible that she trusted Malcolm, but this morning she awoke unharmed, not raped, nor mutilated or murdered. He'd fucked her, yes, consensually. How many times? She wasn't sure if she should count her orgasms or his. And she couldn't count his because he'd fucked her while she'd slept. Had he done it only the one time? Or several times throughout the night? The thought of him gently rutting on her unconscious body aroused her, though she wished it didn't. She had to admit to herself she enjoyed being thoroughly used. It was new information about herself. It didn't trouble her to make this realization. It only troubled her that it didn't trouble her.

Mona laughed.

She laughed because Tou-Tou slept curled in a ball at the end of the bed and she wondered if Malcolm had picked the little cat up and put him there in the night. For in Manet's *Olympia*, a black cat stands guard at the end of his mistress's bed. The black cat symbolized prostitution. Mona had to wonder if the term "pussy" came into fashion before or after *Olympia*.

Tired as she was, Mona would have liked to stay in the bed all day. Unfortunately, the gallery doorbell buzzed. There was work to be done. Always more work.

"Just a moment." Her voice was hoarse as she called out, but the buzzing stopped.

Her body ached in places she'd never ached before and her nipples were ringed with pale blue bruises from his mouth and hands. As quickly as she could, she pulled on her skirt and bra and shirt. Had it all been real? She looked at the bed, the sheets wildly askew and dotted with dried fluid stains. Oh, yes, it had been real. Every sore muscle in her body, especially the ones inside her, told her it was. She went to the side door in the office, the delivery door, unlocked and pushed it open.

"Yes? Can I help you?"

A woman stood across the threshold, dark skin with a white scarf in her hair. She was beautiful as a Raphael, and in her arms she cradled a bouquet overflowing with white roses and baby's breath.

"Delivery for Mona St. James. Is that you, miss?" the woman said in an island accent Mona couldn't place. Something lovely and Caribbean anyway. Had Malcolm found the prettiest woman in the whole city to bring her flowers? She wouldn't put it past him.

"It's me. Thank you," Mona said, taking the flowers from the woman's arms. She should have seen this coming. In Manet's *Olympia*, a woman stands by the courtesan's bed presenting her with white flowers. "Is there a card?"

"Not a card, miss," the woman said. "But he told me to give you this."

She handed Mona a clear glass bottle sealed with a cork.

Mona laughed to herself. Terrible man.

"If you'll wait here, I'll find some cash."

"He tipped me well enough for ten men," the woman said. "Enjoy your flowers. He said you'd more than earned them."

The woman gave her a knowing smile and stepped away. Mona set the flowers on the desk. They smelled of summer, which it was today—June 21st, the summer solstice. A new summer full of promise. She pulled the cork from the bottle. There seemed to be a note inside. It took a little doing to ease the rolled parchment from the bottle's mouth, but at last she worked it out.

Mona unrolled the paper and her eyes widened. She dropped down into her desk chair, heedless of the discomfort.

The paper wasn't a note at all but a drawing. Not a drawing but a sketch—a sketch she recognized instantly. She knew those curves, those watery lines. A sketch of a dancer. Not any sort of dancer. A ballet dancer.

There was only one word on the entire page and one word was all she needed to know Malcolm had made good on his first payment for her services.

Degas.

IV: THE SLAVE MARKET

*M*ona called around to every gallery in town and was given the name and number for Sebastian Leon, a well-respected Degas historian. She took the sketch to him at his apartment on the West Side. When he opened the door to let her in, she was surprised by how young and handsome he was. He couldn't have been more than thirty-five, and the energy with which he greeted her and the sketch was that of an eager schoolboy.

"I couldn't sit still waiting for you," Sebastian said as he pulled her into his apartment. It was a small, intimate sort of place, brick walls painted white with colored framed Degas prints and sketches hung everywhere she looked. He led her to his blue velvet sofa, gave her a glass of white wine, and he sat next to her so close their shoulders touched. "I've been pacing."

He spoke with near childlike enthusiasm. A man who loved art. She liked him already.

"Here it is," she said. "I need to know if it's really his."

Sebastian took the sketch from her, which she'd pressed flat into a leather portfolio. He put on white cloth gloves, opened the portfolio and said, "Ahh…" at the sight of it. "Beautiful." He had curling dark hair, long enough to tuck behind his ears. The curls fell over his forehead as he bent to examine the sketch.

"Have you seen it before?" she asked, looking more at Sebastian than at the sketch.

"Other sketches like it, but not this one. It looks like his lines. Just like it," Sebastian said. He picked up a magnifying glass and examined the signature. He sniffed the paper, explaining that forgeries often had a recognizable smell.

"What do you think?" she asked when he at last placed the sketch into the portfolio and closed it again reverently, like a monk closing his illuminated Bible.

"It's real," he said with a boyish grin. "It's absolutely real. I have no doubt."

"Wonderful," she said. "How much?"

"If it were me—and I wish it was—I'd have it insured for sixty thousand at least."

"I will. Thank you." They clinked their wine glasses in a toast and drank in their happiness.

"I have to ask," he said as she set his glass down on the table. "Where does it come from? You have the provenance?"

"A man gave it to me as a gift."

"A man gave it to you? Simply gave it to you?"

"He'd taken me to bed the night before," she said, wanting to impress handsome Sebastian, perhaps even shock him. "The next morning he had white roses and that sketch delivered to the gallery."

"I don't know who I envy more," he said. "You for having the sketch. Or him, for having you."

Sebastian didn't try to take her to bed, but she sensed he wanted to. Professional courtesy kept him chaste, perhaps? She kissed him goodbye on the cheek, and he told her if her lover had any Degas paintings in storage, she should do whatever he asked to get one. No maidenly modesty in the world was worth more than a Degas painting. Mona promised him that she would do anything she could.

It was a promise she meant to keep.

It took very little time to have the sketch insured, especially with Sebastian Leon's imprimatur behind it. And overnight she was worth sixty thousand more dollars, and all for selling her body to Malcolm. She felt no guilt over sleeping with Malcolm in exchange for valuable art. Although she'd been desperately sore after their night together and had worn finger-sized pale blue bruises on her breasts for a week afterwards, she felt no negative aftereffects. She'd even gone to the nearest clinic and had herself tested for every possible venereal disease and after a tense two weeks of waiting received the results—all negative. Nor was she pregnant, which hadn't concerned her as much since she was on the pill. He was keeping his end of the bargain. Nothing to do but keep hers.

One month passed.

She knew it was time for another liaison when she walked into her office the fourth Saturday evening after her first assignation with Malcolm and found a book of art history on her desk that she hadn't left there. Inside the book was her red velvet choker that Malcolm had taken off her neck while she'd slept. Now it was a bookmark. So this is how he intended to give her instructions on how to wait for him, by showing her a painting? How fitting. How very Malcolm. Last time it had been Manet's *Olympia*. Her hand shook with equal parts nervousness and excitement as she opened the page.

The Slave Market by Jean-Léon Gérôme, 1866.

Interesting choice. Ostensibly it was a painting that showed the horrors of the Near East slave trade. A young girl was stripped naked by her owner in the open market square while men—prospective buyers—gathered round her and inspected the goods on display. One man even held her by her hair and put his finger in mouth to examine her teeth. Horrible, yes. Oh, but titillating too. She'd always thought of it as a teenage boy's fantasy of the slave trade—idealized, romanticized, and eroticized. Imperialistic colonial pornography. Yet the naked girl was beautiful with her golden skin, her dark black hair. Unlike Olympia she was passive, accepting the men's gaze, their touch, their ownership of her without a challenge. She could see why Malcolm would want her in this pose. Would he examine her teeth as well? She'd have to behave herself. The temptation to bite him if he put a finger in her mouth would be almost overwhelming.

So she was to be his slave girl in the marketplace tomorrow night.

Very well. She could do that. Sunday after she closed the gallery, she went to her apartment to nap and to shower and to shave. She arranged her hair as best she could to match the girl in the Gérôme painting. She parted it down the middle and tied it with a purple ribbon at the nape of her neck. Wearing her favorite purple summer dress and sandals, she walked back to the gallery. This time she packed empty glass tumblers she could fill with water at the gallery from the bathroom tap. She didn't want to give Malcolm any more ideas.

He seemed to have enough ideas of his own.

It was near midnight when she returned to the gallery. She was eager to see Malcolm again, and even more eager to see what artwork she'd earn from his collection. At least she told herself all she cared about was earning the art, earning money for The Red. That she enjoyed earning the money was beside the point. And yet, her step was quick and she'd spent half the day checking the clock.

It was time.

She went to the red door that led to the back room, took a steadying breath, and pushed it open. At once she was seized by rough male hands and dragged into the room. The door slammed behind her and she was pushed against it, her back to it. She tried to scream but a hand covered her mouth.

"Quiet, girl."

The words came from Malcolm, though he did not look as he did when she'd last seen him. He'd grown a short beard and mustache, which made him look older, even slightly sinister. He held a rope in one hand. So it was to be role play? Very well. She'd given him carte blanche. Anything meant anything. She shouldn't be shocked or afraid. But she was afraid. She was.

They weren't alone.

With Malcolm's hand over her mouth she glanced around the room wildly in her panic. Four men in suits stood waiting by a wooden box in the center of the room. All four men wore masquerade masks—one black, one gray, one red, one gold. They were cyphers in their masks, anonymous. Only Malcolm was unmasked.

"Is there a problem with the girl?" one of the men called out, the one in the red mask. His tone was imperious.

"Not at all," Malcolm said. "I've got her."

"Let's see her then," the man in the black mask said. He sounded bored, impatient. "We haven't got all night."

Who were these men? She couldn't ask because Malcolm had ordered her into silence and his hand still covered her mouth.

"Coming," Malcolm said. "You won't be disappointed."

He spun her without warning, turning her back to him. He put his mouth at her ear and whispered, "Do not fight me, girl. Put on a good show. I want a high price for you."

A good show... He'd told her last time she existed to entertain him. So be it. She nodded and said nothing, though her heart still raced with terror. Would he let all these men fuck her? No. She knew he wouldn't.

Or did she?

He took her by the arms and pulled her away from the door. He walked behind her, steering her to the center of the room where the four masked men waited. She tried to study their faces but only one lamp was lit, and they were all in shadows. Only the colors of their masks could be clearly seen. She looked at the floor instead.

"On the box," Malcolm ordered and she stepped up onto the low wooden platform. Malcolm bent and pulled her shoes from her feet, tossing them into the shadows. He stood and mounted the platform behind her.

"Let's have a look," the man in the gold mask said and the other masked men nodded their heads in agreement.

Behind her, Malcolm dragged the straps of her purple summer dress down her arms. She wore no bra and she had to force herself not to fight him as he pushed her dress down and let it pool at her feet. In an instant he had a small sharp knife out and he used the blade to cut her panties off her hips and those he tossed into the shadows with her shoes.

She was naked, completely naked, and standing in front of four strange men. Malcolm produced a rope from his jacket pocket and used it to tie her hands in front of her. Then he reached high and she looked up. He'd hung a metal hook from a ceiling beam. With a swift and easy motion that showed he'd done this sort of thing a thousand times before, Malcolm hoisted her hands over her head and secured the ropes on her wrists to the hook.

There was no escape.

Mona wiggled her hands and the men chuckled at the sight of her struggles.

"Here we are, gentlemen," Malcolm said. "Tonight's best lot. Take your time. Bid high. She's worth it."

"I'll be the judge of that," the man in the red mask said as he stepped up onto the wooden platform. Malcolm stood behind her, holding her hair in his hand. Mona panted in fear and anticipation. The red-masked man placed his hand on her quivering stomach and stroked her side and hips.

"Very smooth skin," he said.

"The smoothest you'll find on the market," Malcolm said.

The red-masked man took a hard handful of her thigh and gripped it, slapped it. The men watching laughed again.

"The breasts are particularly fine," Malcolm said. "As you see."

"I see," the red-masked man said.

"I don't," said another man.

"Then come see for yourself," Malcolm ordered.

The man in the red mask stepped off the platform and the man in the gold mask stepped on. Without hesitation he groped her right breast with a large strong hand. Mona cried out more in shock than pain. With her hands tied so high, her breasts were exposed and she couldn't cover them in any way. It was stunning to be touched so intimately by a stranger. He lifted the breast as if to weigh it in his palm, then he pulled the nipple, twisting it a little, teasing and testing it.

"Very nice," the gold-masked man said, nodding. He shifted to the side and did the same to her left breast. He groped it firmly, squeezed it, lifted and weighed it, before pinching the nipple again, tugging it, and letting it go. "How's the ass?"

"See for yourself." Malcolm turned her so that her back was to the gold-masked man. She felt a hand on her backside, rubbing her from her hip to her upper thigh.

"A full ass," the man said, pleased, as he rubbed. "Soft but not too soft." He slapped it once and Mona gasped, gasped again when he gripped it in both hands and squeezed it, then pinched it. "Young firm flesh. My favorite."

"I told you she was worth the money," Malcolm said.

It was unbearable, being treated like this, treated like chattel. She burned hot with shame and humiliation. Tears stung her eyes. Her breathing was labored and her arms ached. She wanted to cover herself so badly.

"We have to see the cunt first," another man said. "You know that."

"Of course," Malcolm said, laughing. "Of course you have to see the cunt."

"Let's see it then."

Mona groaned as Malcolm turned her to face the four men again. Two of them stepped onto the platform, the man in the black mask and the man in the red mask. Each of them took one of her legs in his hands and hoisted her off her feet. They held her thighs open, her feet dangling helplessly in mid-air, her sex open and exposed. The man in the gray mask stepped forward. He didn't stand on the platform. He was at eye level with her vulva.

She shivered and moaned as the man in the gray mask extended his hand and lightly touched her pubic lips.

"Exquisite," he said. "Well-formed."

"Tight too," Malcolm said. "But she can take anything you want to give her."

She saw the hint of a smile on the gray mask's lips. With his thumb and forefinger, he opened the inner folds of her vulva, revealing the hole, the entrance to her body. He slipped one finger into it.

"And wet. Very wet," the man in the gray mask said. It was true. Humiliating but true. For all her shame and fear, she was undeniably aroused as well. The man inserted a second finger into her and spread the two fingers wide in a V. She felt herself opening. It was a violation of the sanctity of her body. Why did she relish it?

"What have we here…" the man said as he pushed his fingertip into a deep hollow inside her, near the pubic bone. He pushed hard into the hollow, poked the hollow, prodded at it, teased the delicate dancing nerves. "I can feel her pulse right here. Very rapid."

"Let me feel it," the man in the gold mask said. She was empty again but only for a moment, as the gold-masked man put his finger into her and found that same little hollow along the back wall. Her head fell back onto Malcolm's shoulder as the man in the gold man fingered and fondled her while she hung in the air, spread out and on display. The man in the gold mask examined her clitoris as well, kneeling in front of her and pulling up the tiny hood of flesh to see the organ. It was swollen and she hated herself for that. She hated it all, hated being held, being opened, being examined and displayed…

Oh, but she loved it too.

As the man in the gold mask continued to spread out and probe her sex, the man in the black mask turned his attention to her mouth. She struggled against Malcolm's shoulder as the man pried her lips apart.

"Don't bite," he chided as he stuck a finger into her mouth. She felt it against her teeth. He was counting them, she could tell. But when he was done, he left his finger pressed lightly against her tongue. Now they'd made her mute. A hand that belonged to someone, she didn't know which man, grasped her breast again and cupped it roughly. A hot mouth latched onto her other nipple and sucked it hard. The fingers worked inside her sex, stroking and rubbing and opening her up wider and wider. She heard the sounds of her own intense wetness. Her labia were pulled and tugged like her nipples, lightly slapped before he, whoever it was this time, pushed his fingers into her again. Three fingers this time, or was it four? She couldn't tell anymore. She was dripping with need. Five men and their mouths and their hands were all together touching her, fondling her, sucking her and penetrating her mouth and her sex as she writhed and moaned softly, unable to protest or cry out or beg for mercy or—even worse and far more likely—begged them to fuck her. She craved their cocks, all five of them. Before, she'd feared Malcolm would let them fuck her. Now she feared he wouldn't. But these were mad thoughts. She couldn't let that happen. She struggled in the iron grasp of the five men, but it did no good, only harm, as the writhing brought her even closer to climax.

Then they all let her go.

It happened so fast, she would have fallen to the floor if the rope hadn't held her wrists. They released her and stepped off the platform as if someone had given a command she hadn't heard. She shivered, suddenly cold. Only Malcolm still stood close. She wanted to press her body into his, but he had her by the waist, holding her in place.

"Well, gentlemen, any other requests?" Malcolm asked. "Are we ready to start the bidding yet?"

She braced herself for the haggling. What were they buying? The right to fuck her? Or was it still part of the game?

"Bend her over," one of the men said. "Let's see all her holes."

"If you insist," Malcolm said.

"I want to know exactly what I'm getting," the man in the red mask said. "If it's no trouble."

"I admire a savvy buyer. And no," Malcolm said. "No trouble at all. I'll put her on the pedestal."

"Very good," the red-masked man said. The other three men murmured their assent.

Pedestal? What sort of pedestal? Malcolm dragged her off the wooden platform and into the shadows. The light followed as one of the men lifted the floor candle and carried it over to the far corner of the room where Malcolm was taking her. She saw something there, something waist high and covered with a large velvet cloth. Malcolm pulled off the cloth and dropped it to the floor. It was a black leather stool of sorts, but wide enough for her to kneel upon easily. Jutting up from the center of the seat was a large thick phallus, smooth black leather and terrifyingly long—a foot long at least. She shrank from the sight of it, but Malcolm didn't allow her to flee. He lifted her off her feet and placed her on the top of the pedestal. He took her hips and angled them so that the tip of the phallus kissed the entrance of her hole.

"Take it," he said, an order she couldn't refuse. Her body wouldn't let her. She went down onto her hands and knees and sank onto the phallus, sliding her knees apart and taking as much of it into her as she could. As wet as she was, the massive object went into her easily and she rocked on it a little to take even more. She felt the muscles giving way to the phallus, accepting it, engulfing it. Malcolm had her pinned like a moth under glass. Pinned and put on display.

"Gentlemen, have a look," Malcolm said. "I have oil here if you need it."

The consummate salesman.

Mona hung her head, hiding her face behind her hair as the first man whose face she couldn't see in this position came behind her and spread her buttocks apart. He made a pleased sound like he liked what he saw. He touched her with a finger and she gasped and shuddered. The fingertip was wet, covered in some sort of thick oil or lubricant. He slicked it all over the little hole, all around it. She tingled at the unusual sensation. It wasn't unpleasant being caressed there on that sensitive opening, wasn't unpleasant when the man slid a single finger into her as far as his finger could go. He held the finger in her, not moving it for a long time. She heard the men talking among themselves, saying things like "Very nice" and "Well done." Inside her she felt the man moving his finger, not in and out, but around in a circle, opening her ever more and more.

"You have a plug?" the man asked Malcolm.

"Of course," Malcolm said.

The finger left her but she soon felt something cold against her, cold and smooth like another phallus but far narrower than the one inside her sex. The man wielding it pushed the tip into her, paused, then pushed it in a few inches more as Mona let out a tense hiss between her teeth. Never before had a lover put anything into her ass—not a finger, not a phallus, not a cock. Yet here it was, going in as if it was made for her body. The man slid it in to the hilt and stopped. The base of the plug would let it go no deeper. Soft moans escaped her lips as Mona's body adjusted itself to being doubly penetrated on the pedestal. She rocked back and forth, fucking herself with the phallus inside her vagina as the four prospective "buyers" walked around her. One stroked her hair, lifted it and sniffed it. Another stood by her face and took her nipples between his fingers and lightly pulled them. His fingers were cold and sent currents of electricity through her breasts and back. Another man played with her clitoris. His fingertip was wet with the oil as he stroked her. The last man rubbed her buttocks, caressing them lightly but over and over again. Sometimes he would pause to touch the plug or the phallus between caresses.

"Now, gentlemen," Malcolm began, "let's start the bidding, shall we?"

"I'll take her for a hundred," the man in the red mask said. A hundred dollars? A hundred thousand? A hundred days?

"Anyone wish to counter-offer?" Malcolm asked.

"Too rich for my blood," the man in the gold mask said. He pinched her nipples again and she flinched as her sex contracted around the phallus.

"Mine too, I'm afraid," said another man. He slapped her thigh lightly as if saying goodbye to prize horseflesh.

"I'd love to take her," the last man said. "But I promised myself I wouldn't spend more than eighty."

"Then I think we have a deal, my good sir," Malcolm said. The man in the red mask had been the one fondling her clitoris. Through the veil of her hair she saw him and Malcolm shaking hands. They moved out of her eye line, stood behind her. "Shall I take her off the pedestal for you?"

"No," the man in the red mask said. "Leave her there. I'll handle it."

She heard footsteps, the door opening and closing, but she was certain the man in the red mask hadn't left her because she felt his finger on her clitoris again. And then on her labia split wide by the huge phallus penetrating her.

"Magnificent," he said. "Worth every penny."

He took her hips in his hands and pushed her down, forcing her to take more of the phallus. Her head came up and she moaned with need. She could barely see. Everything was red. The blood behind her eyes, the blaze of her desire, the engorged flesh of her sex, all red, red everything everywhere, red as the man's mask, the man who owned her. He lifted her up and off the pedestal and put her on her feet. He'd opened his black suit pants and his cock was out, erect and glistening with fluid at the engorged red tip. She had to have it inside her. She had to. She reached for it but he caught her hands, pushed her back into the wall and held her wrists over her head. Desperate, she thrust her hips forward to rub against him. Every move she made sent wild tremors through her body. The plug was deep in her ass still and she wanted it there. But she needed his cock inside her too. Needed it more than anything.

He guided the tip to graze her painfully swollen clitoris and she cried out. With one quick pump of his hips, he pushed the tip through the folds of her labia. With one more pump he penetrated her and with a final pump he entered her entirely. She came off her feet as he lifted her with his hips and pinned her again, this time against the wall. Her breasts bounced as his thrusts lifted her and lifted her. She was nearly screaming in her ecstasy, out of her mind with her pleasure. It felt like she had a rod of iron inside her, as thick, as hot, and as hard as anything could be. She didn't know this man at all but he owned her. He'd bought her body and now he owned her. She was his slave, his possession, chattel, an object, his to do with as he willed. And what he willed was to fuck her against the wall, ram himself deep into her, pound her and pound her until she came with an unholy moan. Her head fell back against the wall and the man in the red mask kissed her neck, sucking the skin there until she felt it break against his teeth. She didn't care. The pain spiked the pleasure. The plug in her ass and the cock in her pussy magnified the orgasm a hundred times. His thrusts were relentless. The man in the mask rammed her once more, twice more, a third time and then she felt the burning seed explode inside her so deep she could swear she could taste it on her tongue.

Mona went limp, but she was still impaled on the man's penis, her feet twined around his thighs, her back pressed to the wall. She rested her head on his shoulder and breathed. Who was this man who'd bought her? What would he do with her? What had she given herself over to? It was wrong, all wrong. She shouldn't be having sex with this stranger, this cypher, this ghost. She put her hands on his chest to push him away.

"Put me down," she said.

"Not yet."

"No, now," she said though he remained inside her, still hard.

"Carte blanche," the man in the red mask said.

"That's for Malcolm, not—"

The man took off his mask. It was Malcolm.

"I told you I liked to play games sometimes," he said with that smile he stole from the devil. "Didn't I?"

"Malcolm…" She stared at him in shock and in horror, still pinned to the wall. "You had a beard."

"Did I?" he asked, lifting his eyebrow.

"You did. Was it…It had to be a fake. You fooled me. I was so sure…" The four men were likely friends of his and when they'd haggled behind her back, Malcolm had taken off his false beard and put on the red mask to trick her. And she'd been tricked, thoroughly tricked.

"You saw what I wanted you to see," he said. "The oldest magician's trick."

"Is this a trick too?" She struggled to free herself from the organ that penetrated her and his body that trapped her against the wall.

"Oh no, this is real. This is the only thing that's real to me," he said. "Come to bed."

He pulled out of her and drew her to the waiting bed, where he threw back the covers and put her on her hands and knees on the white sheets. He stripped out of his clothes and joined her on the bed. Mona shivered with eagerness as Malcolm pushed her hair off her back and kissed her spine from the base to the nape of her neck.

"We won't be needing this anymore," he said as he gently pulled the plug from her ass. She felt far too empty the moment it was out of her body.

"Malcolm…" She made his name a plea. Malcolm positioned his hips behind her and slowly entered her, filling the emptiness inside her. His shaft was wider than the plug but she wanted it inside her more. Mona leaned forward until her head rested on the pillow. Her ass opened up as she bent low and Malcolm was able to enter her fully. She took it all, every inch, and felt a sense of pride that she could.

"You enjoyed being sold and bought," he said as he pumped his cock into her. The strokes were long but not hard, and she could take them easily.

"I hated it," she said.

"You lie. It's fine. I like liars. Lie all you want, my darling. I know you loved it. Your body tells me what your words don't."

"I'm your slave," she said.

"No. You're my employee," he said. "A slave has no choice. But you're here because you want to be. Aren't you? Admit it, Mona…admit you love being my whore," he said as he slid in and out of her ass. No man had ever taken her in that orifice before. Only Malcolm. And only because he'd paid her.

"Never," she said. "Not in a hundred years."

"A hundred years? Is that all?"

"You sold me at auction. You're the devil."

"I'm not the devil, my darling," he said, sinking his teeth into the side of her neck again like some kind of rutting beast. "The devil wants your soul. I only want your body."

He could believe that if wanted, but Mona knew the truth. If he kept fucking her like this, soon enough he would own both.

V: NYMPHS AND SATYR

*M*ona wanted to be angry at Malcolm but it was impossible. Although she'd been frightened by the masked men he'd brought to their liaison and furious he'd tricked her into having sex with a man she thought was a stranger, she couldn't deny she'd never been more aroused in her life. All those men...all those hands...all those mouths on her body...she couldn't think of it without growing damp. Often she'd sneak into the back room, lie on the bed, and bring herself to orgasm with her own hands as she recalled that night, the hands holding her legs in the air while a man she didn't know from Adam plumbed the depths of her body with his fingers. And she could still feel that brutal phallus inside her, pressing against the plug in her ass, the wall of tissue between them quivering and tender. And Malcolm's cock in her ass, she remembered it with such pleasure her nipples hardened with even the slightest recollection of it. Her body buzzed constantly with low-level ardor. If the month didn't pass any faster, she might go mad waiting for him.

The month passed slowly. She didn't go mad.

Instead, she went to an art appraiser to have Malcolm's payment for her night on the auction block authenticated. He'd left a small pastel drawing of figs on the bed, which the appraiser recognized instantly as the work of nineteenth-century Swiss-French painter Jean-Étienne Liotard. She'd almost been hoping for another Degas so she could see Sebastian Leon again. But could she do such a thing? Date a man while her body was promised and sold to another? She was certain Malcolm wouldn't mind her taking another lover. He'd even told her he wouldn't stop her from seeing someone else. Malcolm only required her body one night a month after all. But how would she tell Sebastian about Malcolm? She couldn't, of course, so she did not call him or find an excuse to see him. Her conscience wouldn't allow her. After two nights with Malcolm and his perversions, she was pleased to find she still had a conscience.

On the fourth Saturday after her last assignation, she found the book of art on her desk again.

Poor Tou-Tou. She had to lift the sleeping cat off the book. He loved paper, loved to lie on it and bask or sleep. He whimpered a small feline protest when she moved him off the book cover and into her lap, but he settled there quickly and was soon fast asleep, twitching as he dreamed of mice or birds or something in between.

What did Malcolm have planned for them next? She was almost afraid to look.

But only almost.

She opened the book to the page he'd marked—again—with the red velvet choker she'd worn the night she'd played his Olympia. The painting this month was one by another French artist, William-Adolphe Bouguereau. *Nymphs and Satyr*. Four beautiful, nearly-naked women played on the banks of a halcyon lake. They'd caught a satyr watching them bathe, and now three of the four water nymphs tried to pull the reluctant man-goat into the lake as the fourth nymph waved for the others to join her at the water's edge.

She knew who the satyr was, that was certain.

Mona spent Sunday turning herself into a nymph. She curled her long red hair and put a white flower behind her ear. She found a sheer white nightgown in the back of her closet. Malcolm would surely want her naked, but he could have the pleasure of undressing her himself.

Near midnight she returned to the gallery and entered through the side delivery door. As soon the heavy industrial door latched behind her, she heard music coming from the back room. Music? How odd. It sounded like pan pipes and chimes, playful music, sprightly and light. The score to a satyr's conquest? Perhaps. She carefully eased the door of the back room open…

A hand grabbed her by the arm and pulled her into the room.

"Here she is!" a girl's voice called out. "I found her!"

Mona stumbled into the back room, which had somehow been transformed into a woodland paradise with potted trees and a bubbling stone fountain. The girl who'd grabbed her dropped her hand and joined two other girls, all three in gauzy gowns and long ribbons in their hair dancing about to the music. One girl wore a gauzy gown of yellow, her hair was black and tightly curled and her skin a deep and lovely brown. Another girl wore pink and her hair was white-blonde and her skin as pale as milk glass. Another girl wore a sheer gown of blue and her hair was warm copper and stick-straight and her complexion only a shade lighter.

And she, Mona, was now the fourth girl, with hair of apple red in a gown of white.

Mona was caught up in the dance and the music seemingly came from everywhere and nowhere all at once. Two girls took her hands and soon they were skipping in a circle around the red and golden chair that Mona had loved since her childhood. It had become a throne now, Malcolm sitting naked upon it, his head crowned with laurels. It was a laughable scene, so Mona laughed and the girls laughed too. It was joyous laughter, not mocking, not disdainful. Malcolm's beautiful cock lay half-hard on his lap as he watched his nymphs frolic and dance for him. She hadn't danced in so long, she knew she must look a fool. But it was too pleasant a scene to stop. Her feet felt bewitched by the pipe music and the girls were all so pretty in their gauzy gowns with their hair ribbons flying and their faces all smiles.

"Come dance with us," the girl in the yellow gown said, breaking from the spinning circle and pulling on Malcolm's hand. "Come dance with us, you silly old goat."

The girl in pink gasped and covered her mouth with her hands at the playful insult.

"Silly old goat?" Malcolm grabbed her hand with his other hand and yanked her into his lap. She squealed in surprise and burst into laughter as Malcolm tickled her stomach with his fingers. Mona and the three other girls stood together, their arms locked, watching.

"She'll get it now for sure," the pink girl said, shaking her head.

"She'll wish she hadn't said that," said the girl in blue.

"Or she'll wish she'd said it twice," the girl in pink added and they all laughed, even Malcolm.

"She'll have to be punished," Malcolm said. "Won't you, wicked child?"

"I'm not wicked," the girl in yellow said as she wriggled off his lap. "I'm honest."

"Honestly wicked." Malcolm grabbed her arm again and dragged her back into his lap. "Now kiss me to say you're sorry."

"I won't!" The girl in yellow sounded adamant.

"Then I'll steal the kiss and won't give it back," Malcolm said.

"You wouldn't—" It was all the girl in yellow could say before Malcolm kissed her on the mouth.

The two other nymphs dissolved into girlish laughter at the sight of their friend being kissed by Malcolm. One second the girl in yellow was trying to push him away, the next second she had her hands in his hair, trying to pull him closer. Even Mona laughed, though it was her lover who kissed another. She felt no jealousy. This was the game. The satyr must have his nymphs to torment. The nymphs must have their satyr.

At last the girl in yellow managed to flee from the prison of his lap. She rushed back to Mona and threw her arms around her.

"He caught me," the girl in yellow said. "Don't let him have me."

"You're the one who tried to make him dance with you," Mona said.

"Oh yes," the yellow girl said. She stood up straight and proud. "That was my mistake. And he's still not dancing."

"But we should dance," the girl in blue said. "Let's dance so much he has no choice but to join us."

It made no sense at all to Mona, but nothing in this room with that man and these silly girls did. Even more, she didn't care if it made sense or not. She only wanted to dance with the pretty trio, these gauzy golden-eyed nymphs. They pulled ribbons from their hair and spun like dervishes as the music grew louder and faster. The girl in pink with the milk glass skin and pale yellow hair danced around Malcolm's chair, his throne, and caught her ribbon round his wrist, then used it to drag him to his feet.

"She's hooked a fish!" the girl in yellow shouted. "A big fish."

"That's not a fish, that's a dolphin," said the girl in blue. "See how he grins."

Malcolm leered at the girl in pink who had hooked him. She pulled on the ribbon wrapped round his wrist, but he pulled back—he had his own satyr's trick. She didn't let the ribbon go in time, and he caught her and twined the ribbon round her wrists.

"I'm talking my pet for a walk," he said as he led the girl in pink around the room. "Don't mind us…"

The girl in pink tried to untie herself as she walked behind Malcolm, a pretty puppy on a pretty pink leash. But there was nothing for her. He had her trapped.

"Let me go, beast. Let me go," she said.

He spun her around to face him.

"For the price of a kiss," he said. "I'll think about it."

"He means it, Pinky," the girl in blue said. "Better kiss him or you'll be his pet forever."

"Not that," she said, her cheeks pinking like her name. "Anything but that."

She pressed close to him and tilted her face up, closing her eyes. She was the perfect picture of a martyr. Martyr and satyr. Satyr and Martyr. Silly fools, all of them. Malcolm kissed his pink pet on the lips and the girls in blue and yellow clapped wildly and cheered. Mona did too, for no reason she could name other than it seemed to be part of the game. The kiss continued, deepening. Malcolm bent the girl backwards in his lust. He brought his large right hand to her breast and groped it over her gown.

The girls in blue and yellow booed, but the girl in pink didn't seem to mind. Malcolm's erection pressed between her thighs and was swathed in pink fabric. Red against pink. He yanked the bodice of the girl's dress down, baring her breast. He latched onto the nipple, sucking it into his mouth as the girl trapped in his grasp gave a little cry of pleasure and fear.

"He's got her now," the girl in yellow said. "No getting her out."

"I told her to stay at home today," the blue girl said. "She never listens."

"I never listen either," Mona said, and that made the blue and yellow girls laugh so hard they almost fell over. They took up their ribbons again and skipped in a circle around Malcolm and the pink girl. He had her dress pushed down to her waist now, so that she was naked from the hips up. Her breasts were small and pale and her nipples pink as her gown, and her face was awash in ecstasy as Malcolm licked her little nipples, his hands huge on her tiny waist.

"He's not going to let her go until she gives in," the girl in blue said, taking Mona by the hands and making a bridge with their arms. "Don't you think?"

"I'm sure he'll let her go eventually," Mona said. "Won't he?"

"But she won't be a water nymph when he's done with her," the girl in yellow said. "She'll be a wet nymph!"

Even Malcolm stopped fondling Pinky long enough to roar with laughter. They all laughed and the dancing resumed. They whirled and spun and turned and bowed and it seemed Mona would never tire of it. And in the midst of them, Malcolm tore the blonde girl's pink gown from her body. He turned her around in his arms to take her from behind.

"I knew it," the girl in yellow said as she emerged from a spin. "You can't say I didn't warn her."

Malcolm took his cock in hand and guided it into the girl's pink hole. All the other girls, Mona too, clapped and cheered as Malcolm pulled his captured nymph's hips back against him and rutted into her rapidly. Her wrists were still tied in front of her and she held them to her chest. She gave little sounds of pleasure and protests—oh's and no's and oh's again.

It was a sin to watch and yet impossible to look away. The three free girls huddled together and pointed and giggled behind their hands. Mona felt light as a child, free as a kite. It felt like she'd stumbled into someone else's erotic dream and since she was there, she might as well play along.

The pink girl's face turned red as Malcolm took her even harder from behind. He bent his knees to lower himself a few inches, all the better to ram her deep. His hips undulated obscenely. It seemed his legs were far hairier than Mona remembered and his ears more pointed than ever before. She was dizzy, indeed, from all the laughing and spinning, and she already knew Malcolm could disguise himself in mysterious ways. He made an animalistic sound as he pumped into the girl from behind and the girl let out a girlish whimper. Mona grew wet watching, terribly wet, and she was already eager for her turn with the satyr.

Malcolm's muscles were tight all over his body. He was all sweating skin and straining sinew, organ and bone. He yanked the girl in his grip back against his cock one last time. She cried out in her climax and he grunted in his.

The girl slid off his organ and fell onto the floor on her back.

"Pinky!" the girl in yellow cried. She dropped to her knees at the pink girl's side and took the ribbons from her wrist. The girl in blue lifted the pink girl's pale hand to her lips and kissed it.

"Are you there?" the girl in blue asked.

Pinky opened her eyes and raised her head. "He got me." She gave a pitiful fake cough like a child trying to get out of school for the day.

"In the heart?" the yellow girl asked, her eyes wide with wonder and concern.

"Is my heart between my legs?" the girl, Pinky, asked.

The girls shook their heads.

"Then that's not where he got me!" cried Pinky.

They all laughed again—even Pinky, who was attempting to play dead.

"Baby Blue…" Pinky said through barely parted lips. Her arm lay over her eyes.

"Yes, Pinky?" Baby Blue asked.

"Avenge me…" Pinky said. Her arm fell to the floor and she was gone…for three seconds, until she giggled again.

"I'll get him," Baby Blue said, standing up. "He'll never see me coming."

"Why not?" said the girl in yellow. "Or are you planning on covering his eyes when you come?"

Malcolm crouched behind his throne, pretending to cower as the nymphs plotted their revenge. His dark eyes shifted left and right like he was waiting for an imminent incoming attack from enemies unknown.

"You go left," the girl in yellow said to Mona. "I'll go right. If he tries to run from Baby Blue, one of us can catch him."

"What do we do with him when we catch him?" Mona asked.

The yellow-gowned nymph shook her head. "I haven't thought that far ahead. Let's just get him. One, two, three!"

The three of them raced to the throne.

Mona couldn't wait to get her hands on Malcolm, but he was too fast for her—he spun out of her grasp. He was nearly caught by Baby Blue, but he feinted to the right. Just as the girl in yellow was about to catch him with her ribbon, he clasped her wrist and scooped her up into his arms.

"Oh no!" Baby Blue cried. "He's captured Sunshine!"

"That's impressive," Pinky said from the floor.

"Because she's so fast?" Baby Blue asked.

"Because it's the middle of the night!"

Baby Blue laughed so hard, Mona had to hold her up. Meanwhile, Malcolm had Sunshine, the girl in the yellow dress, on his lap in the throne again. As she wiggled and struggled, he ripped her dress down to her waist—if Mona had to guess, she'd say the wiggling and the struggling did more harm than good. It certainly made it easier for Malcolm to rip her dress, which may or may not have been Sunshine's plan all along. Malcolm pulled her bare back against his naked chest and groped her breasts as he bounced her on his knee.

"Should we try to rescue her?" Baby Blue asked Mona.

"Don't try anything," Sunshine said, her voice quavering as Malcolm bounced her. "You'll only make it worse for me."

"I think she likes it right where she is," Mona whispered.

"She does," Baby Blue whispered back. "But he doesn't need to know that."

Malcolm tore the rest of Sunshine's gown from her body. The gauzy fabric ripped like paper and gathered at his feet like an offering of gold. He lifted Sunshine by her waist, and when he brought her down again it was to impale her on his cock. She took it all at once, her back arching and head tipping backward. Malcolm put his hand on her neck and whispered into her ear.

"What do you think he's saying?" Mona asked Baby Blue.

"Probably something very important," Baby Blue said. Then she giggled again and pulled naked Pinky off the floor and to her feet. While Malcolm dallied with Sunshine in his lap, the three of them would dance. The trio joined hands and spun in circles round the throne. Then they formed a conga line for a few minutes. All the while Malcolm bounced his captive nymph up and down on his lap—lifting her slight weight, holding her in the air and then sliding her down again, impaling her once more and again.

"Let me go!" Sunshine cried. "I demand you set me free!"

"Never!" Malcolm said, all satyr now, his legs hairy as a pelt, his ears pointed as knives.

"Never ever?" Sunshine asked as Malcolm nibbled her neck.

"Not until you come," he said.

She nodded sagely. "Well, I better do that then," she said. He bounced her harder on his lap, making her breasts jiggle and her hair fly here and there. Malcolm fucked her from underneath, bending his hips into hers and sliding her up and down the length of his cock. Finally, his head fell back and he came a foot out of the chair with Sunshine still attached to him, her hips in his grasp as she came and he came and their cries of pleasure mingled into one.

Sunshine slid out of Malcolm's lap, and Mona caught her before she hit the ground.

"Thank you, lady," Sunshine said, smiling up at her in gratitude. "He's a brute, a nasty brute."

"That's not nice," Malcolm said, a pout on his perfect face. "After all I do for you."

"You were very hard on him," Baby Blue said to Sunshine.

"I was not hard on him," said Sunshine. "But he was hard in me!"

Laughter and exuberance were restored. Mona marveled at their playfulness, their lightness, their airiness. They could have been flying kites for all their frivolity. Who knew orgies could be joyful?

All four nymphs danced together as Malcolm watched and clapped in time. They linked arms and changed partners, pirouetted and jeté-ed. Only Mona and Baby Blue were still clothed. Sunshine and Pinky were naked as babes in the wood and didn't seem to mind one bit. The firelight turned

77

Sunshine's dark skin golden and turned pale Pinky red. They were light and lovely as fairies. All they wanted for was wings.

"I suppose it's my turn to face the music," Baby Blue said as she and Mona joined arms for a set in the center of the circle of trees. "Can't put it off any longer."

"Might as well get it over with," Mona told her.

"He's not bad when you get used to him," Pinky told her sweetly.

"No," Sunshine said. "He's worse!"

"Kiss me for luck," Baby Blue said. All three girls pressed soft kisses on her lips. Baby Blue hung her head and slid her feet across the floor as she neared Malcolm's throne with visible trepidation.

"What brings you to me?" Malcolm asked. He crossed a mighty hairy leg over a mighty hair knee. "You have a favor to ask of me?"

"I do, Sir Satyr."

"Name it, girl."

"I ask you to ask a favor of me," Baby Blue said.

"Very well then. I ask you to favor me with your favors," Malcolm said. "Will you?"

She turned around and brought her hands to her mouth. To Mona and Pinky and Sunshine, she whispered, "He's asked me for my favors. How do I say no?"

"You just said no!" Sunshine said.

"Oh, no," said Baby Blue.

"You just said it again!" Pinky said.

"I'd rather hear a yes," Malcolm said.

"Yes, what?" Baby Blue said, turning back around.

"That was definitely a yes," Malcolm said. "You all heard her say yes, yes?"

Mona and Pinky and Sunshine nodded. It was true. She had said yes. What could they do?

Poor Baby Blue. Malcolm bade her to stand before him at his throne and as soon as she did, he tore her dress from her body. Poor Baby Blue. As soon as she was naked, Malcolm took her nipple into his mouth and sucked it while he stroked her between her legs with his fingers. Poor Baby Blue. She had to straddle his lap with her legs trapped by the chair arms so that as soon as he had his cock in her, she wouldn't be able to run away. Poor Baby Blue. She cried and she cried as he held her by the waist and rocked her on his lap, rocking his organ up into her as he suckled at her breasts. Poor Baby Blue. She came so hard and so loud, it must have hurt her tender throat from groaning that hard.

"Was it awful?" Sunshine asked as Baby Blue was finally released from Malcolm's grasp.

"Was it terrible?" Pinky asked.

"It was..." Baby Blue said, shaking her head. "It was...big!"

Then she ran back to the throne and kissed Malcolm on his cheek, stole his laurel crown, and put it on her own head.

"I am now the queen of this courtyard," Baby Blue said. "And I say the next sacrifice shall be..."

She walked to Mona, naked and smiling and serious all at the same time.

"Yes?" Mona asked.

"What's your name?" Baby Blue said.

"She wears white like the moon," Sunshine said. "Shall we call her Moona?"

"That's silly," Pinky said. "She's mad as a loon to be here. Shall we call her Loona?"

"Those are terrible names," Baby Blue said. "I like them both!"

"Call her Moan-a," Malcolm said, his pronouncement straight from the throne. "And we'll see if she earns it."

"Have you ever had this nymph before, Sir Satyr?" Baby Blue asked Malcolm. He shook his head no.

"Then she must be washed in our water first," Pinky said to Baby Blue. "And him too."

"I'll take him," Sunshine said. "You two take our Moona Loona."

The nymphs nodded and shook hands like bankers closing a business deal.

Pinky and Baby Blue took Mona by her hands and drew her to the center of their little indoor grove. In the background, music played, now softer than before. The girls drew her white nightdress down and off her body. They were puzzled by her bra and panties, but soon enough they were long gone as well. It didn't feel strange to be naked—Mona had felt far stranger to be the only one clothed.

On his throne Malcolm watched her intently. Mona would have imagined him done for the night after mounting three young nymphs in a row. But he'd become his character. He was a satyr through and through. His cock, which seemed larger than ever, jutted out, red and proud, from a thatch of thick dark hair. Sunshine knelt at his feet, a large white bowl on the floor and a clay pitcher of water in her hand. She poured the water slowly over Malcolm's organ, using her free hand to wash it with the water.

He was being purified for Mona, and she for him.

Pinky and Baby Blue drew her into in a wide cream-colored basin on the floor. Though she wasn't tired—she had danced and frolicked for what must have been two hours—she was a little overheated. She welcomed the cool clear water they poured over her from her neck to her knees. Pinky poured and Baby Blue splashed the water over her breasts and down her back, between her legs and behind her knees. Then she held out her hands and Pinky filled them with water that Mona drank greedily. She held out her hands again and Pinky filled them. This time, Mona splashed the cold water on her face.

Baby Blue intoned a prayer. "We dedicate this girl into the service of whoever it is or whatever it is we want to service on that particular day."

"We're very pious," Pinky said.

"Pious, yes," Malcolm said. "I shall put her on her knees in piety. Won't I?"

"Will you?" Sunshine asked, still kneeling at his feet.

"I will," he said. "Bring her to me."

"She doesn't want to come to you," Baby Blue said.

"Yes, I do," Mona said.

Pinky glared at her.

"Oh, right," Mona said. "No, I don't want to go to him. Anything but that."

"That's what I thought," Baby Blue said. "But you have to. It's our way."

Pinky and Baby Blue escorted her to Malcolm's throne, all five paces.

"Whew." Pinky ran her hand across her forehead. "That was a journey. She put up a fight the entire way."

"Sit and rest a while," Malcolm said to Pinky and Baby Blue. "You've done well. I'll take her from here."

"He'll probably take her from there as well," Sunshine said, gesturing at Mona's sex. Malcolm reached down and casually tugged Sunshine's nipple. "I deserved that."

"You did," Baby Blue said, and Malcolm did the same to her. "I didn't deserve that," she said, "but I shall bear the injustice stoically."

Malcolm tugged her nipple again and she yelped.

"Perhaps not very stoically," Baby Blue said.

"Silence, nymphs," Malcolm said. "I must see if Moan-a is worthy of being numbered among you."

"How may I serve you, Sir Satyr?" Mona asked, swept up in the game once more. She could hardly keep the smile off her face.

"You may kneel at my feet and kiss the royal scepter."

"What's a scepter?" Pinky whispered into Sunshine's ear.

"It's a prick," Sunshine said.

"It's his prick, Moona," Pinky said. "That's what he wants you to kiss."

"I figured as much," Mona said. She knelt on the floor, her knees sinking into the soft pile of yellow, pink, and blue gauze left behind from the carnage Malcolm had done to the girls' dresses. She took Malcolm's scepter into her hands and rested her elbows on his furry thighs. It felt so real, it all did. The thick hair on his legs and the points of his ears, the warm animal scent of his body. The music didn't sound like it came from a radio or a record. She swore she even saw fireflies flashing in and among the trees of the sacred grove they played in. And the three girls were all impossibly lovely —their youthful ageless faces, their tender breasts, their hairless bodies. They were watercolor nymphs in a watercolor world.

Had all the dancing and spinning and laughing made her dizzy? Was she dreaming?

Perhaps, but she didn't care. She was far too happy in the dream to wake up now.

She pressed a long kiss onto the head of the satyr's cock. Then she opened her mouth and slid the tip between her lips. She tasted his musky flesh, a dash of salt, and craved more of it. Mona ran her hands up his thighs and wrapped her arms around his hips as she sucked the shaft deep into her mouth. Vaguely she heard the nymphs giggling their sweet musical giggles as Mona devoured their satyr lord's prick with her mouth, sucking it all the way to the back of her throat. She ought to have gagged on it, but didn't. She was caught up in the moment, in the fantasy world he'd created for them. She felt she could do anything, even fly if she wanted to—though she would turn down the offer of wings to have her satyr inside her.

"A beautiful new draping for my lap," Malcolm said, as he gathered her hair in his hands, lifted it, and arrayed it all around him so that it draped off his thighs. "Finer than silk, more shimmering than satin, and sucks me off better than any linen ever tried."

Mona beamed with pride, his organ still in her mouth. Her satyr was surrounded by his nymphs. Baby Blue was behind him, placing the laurel crown atop his head again. He turned to Pinky on his right and kissed her lips before turning to the left to lick Sunshine's breast. They all took turns kissing him and he took his turns sucking and licking their necks and breasts, poking his fingers into their wet little cunts, and groping their thighs and their bottoms without apology.

"You make me wish I had four pricks," he said to his nymphs. "I'd take you all at once, my beauties."

"Or we could find three more satyrs," Sunshine said.

"I like my idea better," Malcolm said.

Mona had to stop sucking him simply to laugh. She stroked his prick, catching her breath. After taking the three girls he should have been wilted as a rose in the desert, but under in her hands he was a rod of iron wrapped in warm flesh. She couldn't stop touching him, wouldn't stop even if the world had ended. His scent drew her in—his scent and his power.

He tickled under her chin like a master to his cat. She smiled and set to licking the tip again.

He placed his hands on her shoulders, not pushing her away but massaging her, caressing her. He lifted his hips off his throne to thrust deeper. Mona gripped his thighs hard, holding onto him as he pumped into her mouth, addicted now to the organ down her throat. She had to have it, had to taste it, had to suck it. She was sealed to it and it was lodged in her. The satyr Malcolm groaned in his animal lust, stamping his bare foot on the ground as if the pleasure was maddening. The sound it made was hard and hollow as a hoof on the floor.

His nymphs caressed him, their hands and lips dancing over his skin. Mona heard their whispers: "You can do it, Sir Satyr. You can take it." And Malcolm saying, "No…no…it's too much. She'll kill me with that mouth of hers. She'll suck it right off."

"We'll put it back if she does," one of the girls said. "Who brought the glue?"

And they all laughed except for Mona, who couldn't stop sucking Malcolm off if she wanted to—good thing, then, that she didn't want to stop.

Mona gripped the base of the shaft with one hand and took his heavy testicles in her other. Malcolm growled like a wild beast and stamped his foot again. He writhed under her mouth, moving against his will. Oh, it was dirty, dirty bliss and Mona loved it as much as he did. Her pussy throbbed as if her heart was between her legs, beating and pounding and pumping. She felt Malcolm's hands on her naked back. He clutched at her shoulder blades. She glanced up and saw his head fall back in ecstasy and knew he was there. She sucked as hard as she could, hard enough to make him believe she really would suck it right off. Malcolm roared like an animal again and his body went stiff as a board under her, his hips hovering in the air a few inches off his throne.

Then he came. It was such a surge of hot fluid in her throat, Mona could barely swallow it all. It surged and surged and she swallowed and swallowed. She thought it would never end. It tasted salty as the ocean, but it refreshed her like water from a fountain. When the spurts finally ceased, Malcolm rested on his throne, his head back and his eyes closed and his arms dangling down as the nymphs kissed his fingers. She didn't want to release her hold on his cock. It had all been so delicious.

She looked at him and he blinked and opened his eyes.

He smiled.

"See?" Sunshine said. "It didn't break off."

"That's good," Pinky said. "I forgot the glue anyway."

"Kiss me," he said to Mona, his voice a whisper meant for everyone to hear. Reluctantly, Mona let him slip from her mouth. She rose to her feet and gave him the kiss he had commanded of her.

Their tongues mingled and mated. He took her by the waist and held her in place so that she couldn't escape his mouth on her mouth and the tongue that lapped at her lips and delved into her throat. He seemed to be tasting him inside of her. His majesty's royal scepter was as hard as ever —she felt the bulb of the tip pushing into her belly and she craved it inside her. As they kissed, the nymphs resumed their dancing, hand in hand in hand, weaving around the little trees in a race that seemed to have no end, no beginning, no winner, no loser. Malcolm rose off his throne slowly, not breaking the kiss once. He wound her arms around his neck, lifted her off her feet and brought her down onto his cock. He ran her through with it and she cried in relief as it filled her up to the breaking point.

She was a rag doll, light and limp. He lifted her again, brought her down, slid her up and down the full length of him. His hips bucked into her and she could do nothing but hang helplessly in his herculean grasp as he fucked her. He locked his wrists around her waist, forcing her to bend her back so he could ravage her breasts with his tongue and lips. He suckled and licked her. Mona moaned, earning the name he'd given her. She moaned and whimpered as his mouth clamped onto her breast like he never intended to let it go.

All the while he worked inside her aching orifice. The ache grew and grew as he rammed her and pounded her. He was the predator and she his prey and he devoured her like he had not fed in weeks. Her vagina closed on his penis, trapping it inside her with its wild clenching contractions. They were in a battle with each other, both intent on conquest. But when his semen shot into her, showering her insides, she surrendered to him entirely.

He vanquished her with one final, brutal thrust.

She sagged in his arms and he held her close a moment before releasing her to stand unsteadily on her feet.

"Rest now, my lady nymph," he said, gently pushing her to her knees again. He touched her eyelids like he was bewitching them. Or perhaps, instead, blessing them.

She stretched out on her side on a blanket of gauzy pink and yellow, blue and white. The dance continued around her. Malcolm gave chase to the girls as the music played on. Mona couldn't look away from the sport, even though her body ached for sleep. The nymphs, lush and lovely, were shameless in their nakedness. Malcolm—hard still or hard again, she didn't know—caught one in flight. The girl squealed and laughed as he laid her over the throne arms and coupled with her. She wriggled away from his grasp and once free, turned on him and chased him. One minute he was the pursuer, the conqueror, the ravisher of innocent nymphs. The next moment he was the hare in the field, and the nymphs all red and hungry wolves. It was an orgy of laughter, sensual and innocent and erotic all at once. How had he done it? Who were these beautiful girls? As she watched them fight and copulate, dance and kiss, she loved them all. They were finches. They were foxes. They were fools. And she was one of them. A nymph in a moon-white gown. A creature of myth and mist. A girl kissed by goddesses and mated by satyrs.

Until she woke up the next morning in the bed of the back room, that was.

The sacred grove was gone. The nymphs were gone. Malcolm was gone.

And she was merely Mona again.

VI: A PORTRAIT OF A GENTLEMAN

he only explanation Mona could conjure up to explain the events of that night with the nymphs was that Malcolm was a very wealthy man indeed—which she'd already deduced. Only money could buy the necessary "magic" to turn the back room of an art gallery into a small grove and populate it with nubile young women willing and able to sexually service a man dressed as a satyr. She would have guessed he'd drugged her, but there was no drug in the world that caused hallucinations so vivid and solid that also left the taker of the drug feeling better the next day, not worse. The morning after she'd been sore from the dancing, tender from the intercourse, but invigorated like she'd swam naked in a cool clear blue spring on a burning red August day.

It wasn't easy returning to the real world after her night in the grove. But she did because the real world demanded it of her. Malcolm paid her for her night with the satyr and he paid her well. The payment came in the form of a painted miniature of Queen Victoria, which he'd left on her pillow. It was appraised for another fifty thousand dollars. She was tempted to try to sell it at auction, but knew it would fetch a far better price once she could provide Malcolm's promised unimpeachable provenance.

If that day ever came.

The weeks passed by in a crawl. The gallery kept her busy with shows and launches. A writer of erotic books came and did a reading, which allowed Mona to display many of her mother's strange pornographic paintings out in the open. She sold two of them. It would have done her mother's boho heart good to see the pleasure her collection brought to a younger generation.

All that time Mona couldn't stop thinking of Malcolm. Who was he? Why had he picked her? Why did so much time pass between their assignations? What did he have planned for her next? More nymphs? More auctions? More whoring?

All of the above?

At first he'd come to her once a month, but two months had already passed since the night she played a nymph for him. He'd warned her not to expect him to come often. He didn't seem a capricious man, but he had said the liaisons took much out of him. She imagined him in England with a wife and children he could rarely escape. He paid for women because he wanted a sort of sex he couldn't have in his respectable marriage. It explained why he wasn't ready to give her his last name yet, why so much time passed between dalliances, and why every night they spent together was such a production and lasted for hours and hours.

And hours.

After two long months, however, she wondered if she would ever see him again. But in mid-October, when the leaves turned bright orange and rusty red and the temperature demanded sweaters with skirts and stockings on bare legs, she entered her office to find a book on her desk, the red velvet choker marking the page again.

She smiled. It was about damn time.

This time Malcolm hadn't marked a page in the big white book of art history. The book on her desk was the most recent auction catalog from London. She turned to the page he'd marked and saw what there was to see…and what there was to see was a late eighteenth century portrait from English Catholic artist James Sharples.

Portrait of a Gentleman, Small, Three-Quarter Length, Seated on a Chair, In Hunting Attire, A Riding Crop in His Right Hand.

That was certainly it. She saw a dashing gentleman. She saw the canvas was indeed quite small. She saw the man in the portrait was seated on a chair and that he wore hunting attire and in his hand he held a riding crop.

It was a very accurate title for the painting.

So it was to be the crop this time? He'd warned her of that, too. She'd never had a lover beat her before, consensually or otherwise. Her mother had never spanked her. She'd had her bottom pinched by a boy in a bookshop once, and she was ready to slap him when she saw he was no more than fourteen. She'd gotten her revenge by telling on him to his mother, who'd been drinking tea in the café while her son pretended to look at books. The mother had dragged him from the shop by his ear and Mona had smiled all the while. A good memory but not erotic. She didn't imagine she would enjoy being beaten by a riding crop, but who knew? She never thought she'd enjoy frolicking with nymphs or being sold on the auction block or having a bottle stuffed inside her either. And yet she had enjoyed it.

She'd enjoyed it all.

As Malcolm had given her no instructions for what to wear for their Sunday night assignation, she wore her favorite fall dress of crushed red velvet—ankle length, skin tight, backless. She pinned her apple-red hair up in a chignon and let tendrils fall down her neck. If that wouldn't please a man such as Malcolm, nothing would.

Midnight came at last.

Mona went to the gallery, and spent a moment petting sweet, sleepy Tou-Tou in his bed before heading for the back room. She didn't want to seem afraid, so she opened the door without hesitation.

Malcolm was waiting.

He stood in the center of the back room, his back to her. He'd dressed like the man in the portrait. Hunting attire. White breeches, a green velvet jacket, and brown leather riding boots that clung to his thighs like a second skin. He was magnificent, resplendent, utterly desirable. His hair looked a shade longer and a shade lighter, and it was curled on his head in the consummate Regency style.

In his right hand he held a long wooden riding crop with a leather tip.

Mona ignored the crop. She cared nothing about it. She walked to Malcolm, almost ran, and he took her into his arms and kissed her passionately. His mouth was warm and tasted of spiced wine and cigars. She couldn't stop kissing him.

"Beautiful girl," he murmured against her lips. She wanted to tear off his fine white linen cravat and lick the hollow of his throat. She would have kissed it and bitten it. She would have drunk wine out of it. She hadn't given that hollow a second thought until it was covered and hidden from her view.

"I want you already," she said as she grasped the back of his coat and pressed her breasts to his chest. He kissed the tops of her breasts, swelling out of her dress. He ran his fingertips over those soft swells and she shivered and sighed. Her nipples needed sucking and her clitoris needed licking and her pussy needed his cock. She was pleased they would be all alone tonight, their first time all alone together in months. She had things she must ask him, but she knew she couldn't until he'd spent his lust on her. It would be hours, she knew, if the pattern held.

She could wait.

Malcolm had looped the leather cord of the riding crop over his right wrist, and she felt the tip of it tickling her backside as he kissed her mouth. He lightly scored her back with his fingertips, caressing her skin along her spine, cupping her bottom before tickling his way up to the nape of her neck again. He kissed her earlobe, kissed her collarbone. As he kissed her neck, he pulled the strap of her dress down her shoulder to bare her left breast. He held it in his hand, squeezed it as he kissed her mouth. He cupped it in his palm and looked down, smiling at it like a prized possession.

"So lovely," he said. "So young and ripe." He teased the tender red tip with his thumb, tracing the edge of the aureole. Her nipple hardened quickly. It was a red marble under the pad of his thumb. He toyed with it to make her moan. "Tell me what you feel, Mona. Tell me what I do to your body."

"I feel desire."

"Tell me much more than that. How does your nipple feel?"

"Hard. It feels as hard to me as it does to you," she said breathlessly. "A woman can feel when her nipples are this hard."

"As a man can when his cock is hard."

"Yes, I'm sure it's something like that. When you touch my nipple when it's soft, I feel pleasure. But when you touch it when it's this hard, the pleasure is magnified. Ten or twenty times. It's hard to stand, hard to breathe. I ache, Malcolm."

"Where do you ache, Mona? Tell me everywhere you ache." He whispered the order and kissed the top of her breast. His soft hair tickled the bare flesh of her chest. She would die if he made her wait for him to take her.

"My breasts ache," she said. "They need to be licked and sucked hard. And I ache inside for your cock."

"In your cunt."

"In my cunt," she said. He inhaled sharply as if it aroused him to hear her say the word. "It's not just the cunt. The ache is everywhere. In my stomach. In my thighs. Everywhere you touch me. I ache everywhere, Malcolm."

"Here?" he asked, and flicked his tongue across her nipple.

"Yes." The word came out in a gasp.

"Here?" He slid his hand into the long slit of her dress at the top of her thigh. He cupped her between her legs, cupped her cunt, and slipped a finger into her wet hole. She contracted around it involuntarily. Malcolm flinched and she knew he'd felt it.

"Yes…" she hissed.

"Here?" He kissed her chest over her heart. "Do you ache for me here?"

"Malcolm…you told me not to love you. Don't make me love you."

"But do you miss me when I'm gone?" he asked.

"The things you do to me…I'd never dare dream them, much less do them. And yet, when I'm with you, there is no game I wouldn't play, nothing of my body would I keep from you. You leave me and I go mad with waiting. You leave me and you are my every waking thought and my every sleeping dream. And if I knew when you were returning to me, I would count the minutes until I saw you again." She paused. "No, that's a lie."

"What's the truth, Mona?" His voice was so soft and tender it hurt her.

"I would count the seconds."

They breathed together, looking into each other's eyes.

His mouth closed over hers again and they were locked into a kiss that would seemingly never end.

Then it did.

Malcolm panted. He released her breast and wrapped that arm around her back again, pulling her roughly against him.

"What you feel for me is what I want you to feel tonight," he said. "But you might hate me after."

"I could never hate you."

"Don't say things like that," he warned. "Men like me take statements such as that as a challenge."

"Will you beat me very brutally tonight?"

"I will."

"Will I like it?"

"If you let yourself."

"I'll try," she said, scared but willing. Anything for Malcolm. Especially tonight. She'd never met a man who conformed so closely to her ideal. She felt the smooth leather of his riding boot against her bare calf. She rubbed her leg against it like a cat rubbing its cheek against a chair leg it wanted to mark. She ran her hands down the velvet of his broad back, cupped his firm backside and held it while he kissed her. Of their own accord her hips pushed into his again and again. Her sex was already open for him, wet and slick, hollowed out and waiting. If he put his cock into her right now, she'd come before he'd even bottomed out inside her on the first stroke.

But he didn't take her.

"Listen to me, Mona." He put his hands on her neck, lightly cupping it, his thumbs pressing into the hollow of her throat to force her to pay attention to his words. She dropped her hands to her sides and met his dark flinty eyes again. "You'll be mine tonight in a way you've never been mine before. It's one thing to allow a man to pleasure you. It's quite another to allow him to hurt you. You'll know real powerlessness tonight, real fear, true pain. And I will drink it like wine."

"You like my pain?"

"I love your submission to pain. It's human nature to race toward pleasure and flee from pain. That you would fight your own nature to please me by suffering my crop arouses me more than anything you've done for me before."

"I want to please you." She placed her hands on his trim waist, feeling the heavy brocade cloth of his vest and the heat of his body under her hands. "After all, that's what you're paying me for."

"Oh...you will be beaten for that." He eyes narrowed and she saw he meant it.

"Good," she said. "If I'm going to be beaten, I want to have earned it."

"You earned it when you crossed the threshold. You earned it when you sold your body to me." He stepped back from her, putting breathing room between them. She already felt cool without the heat of his body against hers. "Show me my property. Show me what I got for my money."

Mona slipped the other strap of her gown off her shoulder and lowered the bodice. She gathered the fabric in her hands at her waist and pushed it all the way to her ankles. Naked but for the red high heeled shoes she wore, she stepped out of the dress and onto the floor.

"A blank canvas," Malcolm said as he walked a circuit around her naked body. "I'll enjoy painting you red and blue."

She quaked in her shoes with fear and arousal. She'd never been with a man as beautiful as Malcolm and she would have walked barefoot across a pit of red coals to please him tonight...but he was right. Reason called to her, telling her to run from the pain.

She ignored its voice. It sounded too much like her own. She'd far rather listen to Malcolm's.

"Put your arms behind your head," he said. "Clasp your fingers and keep your elbows open. Like a butterfly's wings."

She did as she was told. The move made her arch her back, thrust her breasts forward. Malcolm stood before her, inspecting her.

"Legs wider," he said. He touched the floor with the tip of the riding crop in two places—here and there, showing her where to place her feet. She moved her feet wider apart, a foot and a half, and stood quivering in place.

"Very nice." Malcolm raised the crop and tapped her left nipple with it. Then her right. He caressed the underside of each breast with the triangle of leather on the crop's end. He ran the shaft of the crop down the sides of her body from each elbow to each ankle and back up again. It tickled and made her shiver. She would have given anything to feel Malcolm's body against her right now. She craved it and with every passing second she craved it more. No doubt this was the intention.

He stepped close again. It was torture to be so close without touching. He brought the crop up between them and pressed the flat side of the tip to his lips. Then he pressed the opposite side to her lips.

"Think of it as a kiss," he said when the leather lay against her mouth. "That's all it is. Just a kiss from me to you."

"Most kisses don't leave welts," she said. "I prefer French kissing."

"Well, I'm English. This is English kissing."

Then stepping back again, he brought the crop's leather tip between her legs and lightly tapped her sex. He turned it on its side and used the edge of the tip to pry her apart along the seam of her vulva. She felt the stiff leather corner against the entrance of her body.

"It stings more if it's wet," he said with his devil's grin and for a split second she wondered...what if Malcolm was the devil? With a riding crop in her cunt, she could almost believe it.

So what if he was? She wanted him all the same.

He dipped the riding crop's tip into her sex again, wetting it with her own fluids.

"Insult to injury," she said.

He held his arms wide, smiled, and bowed. "The name of the game, my darling."

She nodded her acquiescence.

"Here are the rules," he said. "You survive my crop, you earn my cock. A hundred strikes of this." He lifted the crop into the air. "For a hundred strokes of this." He pointed casually at his crotch and she could see the outline of his erection through the pale breeches. The trousers adhered so tightly to his body she could even see one long vein running from the base along to the shaft to the tip. She knew that vein. She'd licked it with her own tongue.

A hundred strokes of his cock? She'd come after the first ten, if not on the very first.

"Count for me," he said. "Starting at a hundred."

He stood behind her and she braced herself. What was he waiting for? Was he torturing her with suspense? Taking his aim?

"Admiring the view," he said as if reading her thoughts. She blushed hot at the flattery and smiled. Then he wiped the smile off her face with one quick crack of the crop. It struck high on her thigh in a spot she'd never associated with agony before. It burned like Greek fire.

She cried out in shock and Malcolm laughed.

The bastard *laughed* at her.

"Count, dear," he said, his voice chiding.

"One hundred."

"Did it hurt?" he asked, tenderly touching the burning welt on her thigh.

"Yes," she said.

"I'm sorry, darling." He kissed his fingertips and touched them to the welt. "So very sorry."

Then he kissed her lips softly and massaged her nipples. She moaned in the back of her throat. Her body was a carnival of sensations—the stinging pain, the swelling of her breasts, the tingling of her lips as he kissed her. Her head spun. Did he want to hurt her? If so, then why apologize and kiss her to make up for it?

"There we go, love," he said. "Only ninety-nine to go. Don't feel too bad. When I was fifteen, I was caught buggering my neighbor's lady wife. I would have traded my left ball for a punishment like this."

"Were you beaten?"

"I was."

"With a crop?"

"A bullwhip."

She gasped.

"Like I said, it could be worse. So count your blessings when you count my kisses."

He struck her again with the crop, kissing her hip this time.

"Ninety-nine," she said through the pain.

"Such a good girl," Malcolm said, hitting the side of her neck over the pulse point. "Beautiful and brave. You can't know how much you please me…"

He struck her again, out of nowhere, right on the back of the calf. Her leg almost buckled from the shock and the pain.

"Malcolm—"

"It's all right…" He put his arm around her to hold her up. He cupped her chin in his hand, tilted her face up to his and kissed the tip of her nose. "It's not so bad, is it?"

"No," she said. In his arms, it wasn't so bad. It wasn't so bad at all.

He struck her again. Mona closed her eyes as the pain washed through her. It wasn't unbearable, but it wasn't pleasant either. After a few dozen strikes, it might very well become unbearable, however.

Yet nothing would allow her to break before she'd earned what she wanted and what she wanted was him.

He walked around her body, striking her with the crop high and low—on her thighs, on her stomach, on her breasts, on her backside, so often and so hard she knew she'd hardly be able to sit in a chair tomorrow. But what did tomorrow mean to her when she wasn't certain she'd survive tonight?

The crop didn't sting like a bee. It bit like a snake. Its fangs were sharp and burning and left sharp and burning bite marks all over her body. Malcolm was the snake-charmer and she was mesmerized by how he made the crop dance. He would twirl it in his fingers, casual, playful. Then he'd catch it quick, so fast she couldn't see where the blow would come from and where it would land.

It would have been easier for her to close her eyes tight and pretend it wasn't happening, wait it out, hide inside her mind. But she couldn't. Malcolm wouldn't allow that. After each strike he paused to kiss her, to fondle her breasts and nipples, to massage her hips and quivering belly. After each strike he'd tell her how beautiful she was. He'd tell her what a brave, brave girl she was. He'd tell her how aroused she made him with her submission to his crop. He'd kiss her on the mouth, before suddenly stepping back to strike her once more. Then the cycle would begin again. The crop, the pain, the tender words and tender kisses. Soon she was craving the crop because each strike meant a kiss.

Before he'd begun, a hundred hits sounded like a hundred too many. But each strike earned such affection from Malcolm, such compassion, such sympathy that she was starting to think one hundred wasn't nearly enough. He was forcing her to fall in love—not with him, but with the crop.

She was in love with the crop. The crop, and Malcolm's tender sadism.

And Malcolm too, of course. How could she not? He was inhumanly attractive. His eyes were so black and the room so dark she couldn't tell the iris apart from the pupil. As he shifted this way and that to keep her guessing, the muscles in his thighs tensed and shone through his breeches. His boots sported gold buttons at the tops and she wanted to kiss them for some reason. The thought wouldn't leave her head. She trained her eyes on them, on the glinting gold coins, and let them anchor her into the moment.

"You're staring at my boots, love. Tell me why," he said. He took her in his arms and held her close against him. The crop dangled from his wrist as he ran the flat of his hand down her brutalized back.

"I like them." She panted between the words. Pain suffused her body. Her flesh smoldered like a hot sidewalk in the rain.

"I'm very glad you do. What do you like about them?"

"The gold buttons," she said. "I can't stop looking at them."

"I'll tell you what, my darling girl," he said. "If you can take ten strikes in a row without me stopping, I'll let you kiss those buttons on my boots. What do you think? Would you like that?"

"Very much," she said.

"What do you say to me?"

"Thank you, Malcolm."

"That's very nice, yes. Could you call me sir? I think I'd like to hear it from you. Everything you say sounds so pretty."

"I'll say anything you want, sir."

"Oh, that is even better than I thought it would be. Excellent. You've made me so very happy tonight." He pressed a soft kiss to her lips once more. She would never tire of his kisses or his words of affection or his pride in her. How had she ever lived without this in her life? Without the crop and the counting and the pain that earned her such rewards, would she have eagerly signed up for a thousand strikes of the crop for the next thousand years?

"Are you ready, dear? Only ten. I know you can do it. I know you will do it—for me, won't you?"

"Of course, sir," she said, and her heart welled and she could have wept with love for him. What wouldn't she do for him? Nothing. The answer was nothing. She would take his English kisses over French kisses any day.

She took a breath in and braced herself. Her hands were still on her head. Her arms ached but she didn't care.

When the strike came she was ready. It hit her on an unmarked patch of flesh on the side of her hip. The second strike came right after, in the very same spot. And the third. And the fourth. It was agony by the fifth, terrible agony by the sixth, screaming agony by the seventh. And the eighth and the ninth and the tenth passed in a haze as she wept and shook.

Malcolm caught her in his arms again as she swayed on her feet. "I've got you," he said. "You're safe. You're with me."

She rested her head on his shoulder as he stroked her hair. She put her arms around his neck and he let her.

"I know that hurt, didn't it?" he asked and she nodded. "I'm sorry. You're doing so well though."

"It hurts so much," she said. "I didn't know it could hurt that much."

"You're taking it like you were born for the crop. I wish I had a hundred men here to watch and see what a prize you are. I wouldn't sell you to the highest bidder, not for all the money in the world."

She needed to hear that. It was a balm to her soul. "Thank you, sir," she said.

"Here," he said. "This might help a little."

He put the crop's strap around his wrist again and slipped his hand between her legs. He stroked her labia and clitoris while she clung to his shoulders to steady herself.

"Isn't that nice, love?" he asked.

She nodded against his shoulder, looking down to watch him touch her. She was hot between her legs, hot inside. When he stuck a finger up and into her, she gave a little cry of pleasure.

"That's my girl." He spoke to her like she was a child in need of soothing. So caring. So kind. It was easy to forget that he wasn't simply the solace for her suffering, he was the cause of it. And she loved the suffering as much as the solace. What had he done to her?

"Can I come, sir?" She wanted to climax very badly. She could take more pain, if only she could come. Already his fingers were bringing her close. And his hands were so well-proportioned and muscular and lovely that she could rest her head on his shoulder and watch him touch her sex all night and all day.

"Can you come?" He chuckled lightly even as he wiggled his finger inside her. "What sort of question is that? No. Not yet. You know it's not time yet, silly girl."

"I'm sorry, sir."

"It's fine. It's fine," he said soothingly. "I know it's hard, but you're doing so well. I would hate for you to give up already."

"I won't give up."

"That's the spirit." He grinned at her and tickled her

inside to make her laugh. "Now I believe you've earned a treat. Haven't you?"

"If you say I have."

"And I say you have." He stopped touching her, but that was for the best. She was almost ready to orgasm. If she did, she knew she'd be in terrible trouble. Even worse, she would have disappointed him, and she couldn't live with herself if she disappointed him. Not that. Anything but that.

She slowly sank down to the floor, using his body—so solid and sturdy—to steady herself. Once on her knees, it was near torture not to unfasten the falls of his breeches and take his cock into her mouth and suck it. But that wasn't what she was here for, even though he was stiff and straining so hard against the white fabric she saw it throbbing. She rested her head for a moment against his rock hard thigh and sighed with indescribable pleasure when Malcolm caressed her hair.

"My Mona," he said. "My darling."

She touched the side of his calf and stroked the leather of his boot from his ankle to his knee. It was smooth and supple and she couldn't get enough of it. The two gold coin buttons glinted in the candlelight. First she kissed her fingertips and pressed the kiss to the buttons. Then she brought her lips down to the them and kissed them with her mouth. Malcolm shuddered. She felt it go through his body and into hers. She kissed his boots again, kissed the gold buttons, kissed the leg of the boot that was warm from the heat of his body. While she was on the floor on her hands and knees, Malcolm caressed her sex again with the tip of the crop. She spread her legs wider for him and arched her back, offering her cunt up to him.

He struck it with the crop.

She screamed in sudden agony even though she knew he would do it, even though she wanted him to do it.

"Count, love," he said. "You know you have to count."

"Forty-nine," she said. She'd survived fifty-one strikes already and that last one was worse than all of them combined.

"We're over halfway there," he said as she rested her head against his thigh again. "You've made it so far and so well. Are you tired?"

She nodded and whispered, "Yes, sir."

"I know you're tired." He reached down and lightly brushed her lips with his fingers, lightly teased her cheek with a lock of her own hair. That made her smile. "There's my girl. So obedient. She's even smiling."

"Why do you do this?" she asked, so torn between loving the crop and hating it, loving him and hating him. "Why, sir?"

"I do it out of kindness, of course," he said. "You understand that, don't you?"

She thought of his kisses, his sweet words, and the caring way he touched her welts. He was a kind man. Who but a kind man would give her such affection, such tender concern with her pain?

"I understand, sir. You are very kind." It made her smile to say it, not because it was a lie but because it was true. She understood it all now.

"Now only forty-eight more. Do you want to take them on the floor or would you like to stand again?"

A choice. How kind of him.

"The floor, please, sir."

"If you like," he said. "On your hands and knees. You'll be more comfortable that way. Legs wide. There. Just lovely. I love to see you like this," he said, standing behind her. She knew he was looking at her open and exposed holes. She wanted him to see them. She wanted him to see what he owned. "I'm so very glad I asked you to play this game with me."

"It's my pleasure, sir."

"Oh, I know it is, but it's so rare to find such an eager partner. In truth, my dear, you're really doing me a favor."

She looked up and he had his hands on his chest. So well-mannered. So refined. So civilized. The very portrait of a gentleman indeed.

He took the crop in hand and struck her under her ribcage so hard she went momentarily blind.

He was an angel of beauty and pain.

"Count, darling," he said. "Otherwise I'll forget my place and we'll have to start all over. I hate losing my place, don't you?"

He was the devil incarnate.

"Forty-eight," she said through gritted teeth.

"That's right. Almost there. Carry on. That's my girl."

Angel.

"Oh, that hurt my hand so I know it must have hurt you. I'm so sorry, my darling."

Demon.

On and on it went. The hits followed by words of encouragement and affection followed by more hits. Mona grew dizzy. It was hard to keep count but unthinkable to lose count. What if he started over? What if he didn't? Even as she counted, it seemed time had stopped. The clock stopped. The world stopped. They had always played this game and they always would. That was how it should be. Heaven and hell were in this room and they had one foot in each.

"Only ten left, sweetheart. You're amazing, you know. Simply amazing at this."

She counted the last few strikes and by the final five she'd curled into the fetal position on the hardwood floor. Two left. Just two.

"Darling?" Malcolm's voice penetrated the fog of her suffering. "My angel girl?"

"Yes, sir?"

"You need to lie on your back for me. All right?"

She whimpered in pain as she unfurled herself from the self-protective cocoon she'd rolled herself into. Every movement left her body in misery. She felt like an old book that hadn't been opened in centuries and now someone had come at last, taken the book from the shelf, broken the spine and riffled through pages that had been pressed together so long their ink had turned to glue. Sinews screamed. Muscles moaned. Simply lying on her back had made her weep again. Hot tears poured from her eyes, stealing her peripheral vision, though Malcolm remained in perfect focus. He straddled her at her hips with those boots of his she worshiped, one leather ankle pressed against each side of her body.

"Perfect," he said. He looked her up and down, one hand on his chin and the other on his hip the way he had been the first night she'd seen him. He perused her like the work of an old master. "Wait, not quite. Put your hands behind your head again. I want you to cradle your head. The floor's so hard, I would never want you to hurt yourself."

She loved him for his concern. Had she ever met a man more thoughtful? She placed her hands behind her head and cradled her head in her palms.

"Marvelous." He smiled down at her. "Now two more to go. We can do this together. Ready, my sweet?"

"Ready, sir."

"I haven't the words to tell you how much I've enjoyed this," he said. "I simply don't have the words."

He raised the crop and lashed it down, striking her right breast so hard she screamed, so hard she heard the swish of it in the wind like the sound of a whip.

She coughed from the pain and it was the greatest test of her willpower to choke out the number.

"Two," she said, more tears burning her cheeks.

"Last one, darling. Then we're all done. And won't that be lovely?"

He lashed her again, one final time, striking the side of her left breast. She cried out the last number of her torment and rolled again onto her side, burying her face in her hands to weep.

Far away she heard movement—the rustle of fabric, boot heels on the hardwood. When she'd worn herself out with weeping, she continued to lay there, spent from her suffering and yet strangely peaceful. Though it was all over, the memory of the words Malcolm had said to her during her beating rang in her ears like the chiming of a golden bell.

You're the bravest girl in the world.

My princess, my angel, my darling, my dear.

You're lovelier like this than I've ever seen you.

You can't know what this means to me, what a gift you've given me tonight.

You please me beyond words, Mona.

She heard those words in her ear again, because Malcolm spoke them again. He had come to the floor and taken her in his arms. He lifted her up, holding her like a babe in arms, all the while whispering his admiration of her, his adoration. She put her arms around his strong shoulders and held him as he carried her to the bed. The velvet of his coat prickled against her savaged skin, yet she relished the sensation since it meant he was holding her.

"Here we go," he said, laying her on the bed. He'd pulled the covers back so she lay on the soft white sheet. For all its softness, she still winced as her sore body met the mattress.

"I know it hurts." Malcolm sat on the bed by her side and took her hand in his. He kissed her wrist, kissed her palm, and all five fingers received their own kisses. Her knuckles too. "I'm so proud of you, dearest."

"Did I please you?"

"More than I can ever say."

He kissed her forehead, kissed her eyelids, kissed her lips.

"Stay there," he said. "I'll tend to your wounds."

"Will you make love to me?"

He smiled, laughed softly. "All night long," he said. "But first I must take care of you. Your well-being is more important than anything else. You know that, don't you?"

These didn't sound like lines from the play they were acting out. Important to him? How? Why? She was his whore. That was all, wasn't it?

"Am I important to you?" she asked.

He brought her hand to his lips again, pressed it to his mouth, and closed his eyes.

"I have waited a very long time for you," he said. "And tonight you've proven to me just how very special you are." He put her hand onto her chest and kissed the back of it. "Rest here. You've earned it."

Mona feared to look at her own body, but she did so anyway. She wanted to see what Malcolm saw. Upon lifting her head, she winced. In stripes along her thighs, and in patches on her stomach, and in whorls on her arms and breasts, she saw deep red welts. Some were pure scarlet red. Others a rusty red with black or blue cores. She imagined her entire backside from her neck to her knees looked about the same.

She wasn't horrified by what she saw. In truth, she found the welts erotic, because Malcolm had trained her eyes to see kisses where others would see wounds.

Malcolm set the wooden chair next to the bed and on the seat of the chair he placed a bowl of water.

"Only water," he said. "Warm water, not hot. Lie still for me."

She nodded and laid her head back on the pillow. For him. He'd said to lie still for him and for him she would lie still. For him she would move. For him she would live and breathe. For him.

He brought his hands to his throat and unfastened the white linen cravat. He unwound it from his neck and at last there it was, the hollow of his throat, the hollow she'd craved to kiss and lick and worship. She smiled, happier than she'd been in years. He folded the linen into a thick square and dipped it into the bowl of water. Then he wrung it out, flattened it out, and pressed it against one of the screaming red and black welts on her hips. She hissed through her teeth. But soon the pain dissipated and the warmth permeated her skin and sunk into the deep layers of tissue, soothing her down to the bone.

"Better?" Malcolm asked. She gave him a tired smile. He dipped the linen into the water again, pressed it to another welt where it quieted the screaming of her skin. For a long time, he ministered to her wounds. Not a single one was missed. When he finished with the front of her body, she rolled onto her stomach and rested her cheek against the pillow. He'd asked her if she knew how important she was to him. No, she didn't know. But she felt it. The way he tended to her welts, to her needs, with such solicitude was beyond anything she'd experienced from a lover before. She felt spoiled as an only child, treasured as a prized possession, doted on like a king's most favored concubine. What magic was it, what sorcery that could turn an act of violence and pain into an act of adoration and affection? It was alchemy, the art of turning base things into gold.

"Would you give me permission to love you, sir?" she asked Malcolm.

"You may tonight," he said, the slightest smile on his lips to show how secretly pleased he was. "You won't love me next time I come to you, so enjoy it while you can."

She laughed softly into the pillow. Hard to take such a

threat seriously from a man who was using his own linen cravat to tend to her wounds.

"I don't believe that," she said.

"What did I warn you about saying things like that?"

"I know, I know, sir. Men like you take it as a challenge."

"You only love me tonight because of the beating. You understand that, don't you?"

Before tonight, she would have said "no," that made no sense, there was no logic to it. He'd done something to her mind as well as to her body. By the end of her beating, she couldn't tell the crop apart from his kindnesses. They were one and the same to her so that every strike of the crop was tender as a kiss and every word of tenderness made her crave the crop.

"Now I understand," she said, because now she did.

When he'd finished with the water, he brought out a clear glass bottle of golden oil. It smelled like crushed wildflowers and warmed her skin even more as he rubbed it into her sore flesh. He massaged her entire body—back and legs, shoulders and arms—then bade her roll onto her back again so he could do the same to her front. He lingered long over her breasts, using both of his hands on each one. She gave herself up to his hands, let him mold her like clay. She had no will over her own body. She willed only that Malcolm's will be done.

Malcolm slicked the warm oil all over her stomach and hips and thighs. He brought his hand between her legs and nudged her thighs open. He glazed her clitoris with the oil and stroked circles all around it. It swelled under his touch and pulsed against his finger. She felt that deep delicious hollowness inside her again. He filled it with his fingers when he slid them up into her sex, the oil allowing him deep penetration. It was bliss to spread her legs far apart for him so that he could have his way with her. She watched as his fingers disappeared inside her body one by one, probing and parting her from within. Mona panted through her nose. She knew she mustn't come until his cock was inside her. If he didn't put it there soon she'd be forced to beg him for it.

"Do you have children?" she asked.

He laughed softly. "I have four fingers in your cunt and you're asking me if I have children. Do you think I'm checking to see if there's room for one more?"

She grinned broadly, too tired and aroused to laugh.

"I only wondered," she said.

"Does it matter to you?" he asked.

"I'm nosy. And you're a mystery."

"I have children, yes. Though not so young anymore."

"Do you love them?"

"I love them though they've disappointed me."

"How so?"

"They're...respectable," he said. "Respectable and well-behaved. Good citizens of the realm. They're boring. Except the youngest. He takes after me." His words made her grin drunkenly. "Are you happy to know that?"

"I am," she said. "Although...I don't know why."

"You're open," he said.

"I know I am."

"Not like that though..." He glanced down at his hand that was in her cunt up to the thumb. "I broke you open tonight. Up here." With his free hand he tapped his temple, indicating his mind. "And here." He tapped his chest over his heart. "You feel close to me."

"I do," she said.

"It's the intimacy of captor and captive. There's nothing like it."

"Am I your captive?"

"You are tonight."

"Can you keep me forever?"

"I wish I could," he said, and she believed he meant it. At least tonight he meant it.

"But you can't?"

He shook his head. "But…if you want, you can keep me."

"What does that mean?"

His smile turned him back into that handsome devil she knew and loved.

"You'll see," he said. "Now close your eyes and keep them closed."

She didn't want to obey this order; it was too enjoyable to look at him. But she couldn't refuse him. Mona closed her eyes and relaxed into the soft sheets. She heard the brass headboard rattle as Malcolm slid his body on top of hers. She sensed movement but kept her eyes closed even as she felt him crawling up the bed, over her. First he removed her pillow and laid her flat on her back on the bed. He then lifted her arms and put them over her head. Her arms were slack, her entire body loose and yielding. He was twining the linen cravat around her wrists, securing her to the brass slats of the headboard. Never before had she engaged in bondage with a lover. She should have guessed Malcolm would be her first. She heard fabric rip as Malcolm moved off of her and to her ankles where he used the other half of the cravat to tie each of them to the slats of the footboard. Nothing about being restrained by him scared her. Quite the opposite, she felt swaddled and secure. It was restful to be tied spread-eagle to the bed. She was absolved of all responsibility, absolved of all sin. What could she do? Nothing. She could only lie there passively as he did whatever it was he wanted to do to her. And whatever he wanted to do with her was what she wanted done.

Malcolm crawled over her again. She felt the naked tip of his cock graze her stomach. Her vagina contracted in hungry need for it. But he didn't move down and push it inside her like she wanted. He straddled her head instead.

"Open your eyes," he said, and when she did it was to find him holding the dripping tip at her chin. He didn't have to tell her to take it into her mouth. He placed his hand under the back of her head and lifted it with all the gentleness of a nurse raising the head of a sick patient to drink some water. She did it willingly, wrapping the tip with her lips and sucking. A small burst of semen shot into her mouth and she swallowed it eagerly. It was merely a taste of what was to come. He'd been erect for well over an hour now. Surely he was as ready to orgasm as she was. He slowly fucked her mouth. The only thing more erotic than the taste of him on her tongue was the feel of his leather boots against the sides of her breasts. As much as she relished his naked body, she was pleased he'd kept his clothes on, baring only the organ he needed to fuck her. He was resplendent, and she wanted to know what it was like to be ridden by a man who wore boots for the job in question. God, he had turned her into a whore, hadn't he? A whore with no shame in her whoring, that's what he'd made her. He'd cracked open something in her, some dormant, latent proclivity for pain and punishment and being treated like a possession. She could never go back to the way it was before. Whatever it would take to keep him in her life, she would do it. This devil, this angel, this man. She almost wanted him to make her pregnant. It would be a tie to him, a tether. She pushed the thought from her mind. These were dangerous dreams. What had he done to her?

At this angle she couldn't do much more than lick and suck the tip, but she gave it the full measure of her attention and adoration. She worshiped the organ in her mouth. She served it and its needs, its desires, its wants and thanked it that what it wanted tonight was her.

Malcolm had one hand on his cock as he guided it in and out of her mouth, one hand atop the brass headboard. She loved to hear his ragged breaths. He sounded like he was close to his breaking point. She craved his semen, wanted it inside her—any hole would do. But he kept fucking her mouth, not coming, torturing himself with pleasure as much as he'd tortured her.

Mona sucked it as deep as she could, pulling on it with her mouth, and Malcolm let out a groan of abject ecstasy.

"Fuck…" he breathed and Mona would have smiled if her mouth wasn't otherwise occupied.

Malcolm slowly eased himself from her mouth and moved down her body until his knees straddled her hips.

"Wicked girl," he said. "You almost made me spill all over your face."

"Oh no," she said. "Anything but that."

"You modern girls are so hard to scandalize."

"Is that what you're trying to do?" she asked. "Scandalize me?"

"Is it working?"

"You've turned me into a whore and made me happy about it. Consider me thoroughly scandalized."

He chuckled and it was a sinister mad scientist sound. "If you think you're scandalized now…wait until I'm done with you."

She said nothing to that because she never wanted him to be done with her.

Malcolm lowered his head to her right breast and suckled lightly. She closed her eyes and rested her head back, basking in the bliss of his mouth and the pull and tug on her nipple. It sent rings of heat and pleasure radiating through her chest and stomach, making her inner muscles clench again and again. Her entire sex dampened and stirred, eager for him to enter her. He seemed in no hurry to take her, so she laid there helpless to do anything but enjoy herself. His mouth moved to her other nipple. It hardened as he lapped at it. The aching of the welts had quieted. Before they had screamed at her, but now they merely whispered reminders they were there. The wounds made her very aware of her body. Whenever Malcolm touched one of her welts or bruises, on purpose or by accident, she remembered the kiss of his crop, those words that had melted her down and recast her into a new image. She remembered his twin gifts of pain and tenderness, and she loved him for both.

Without a word of warning, Malcolm lowered his hips and pressed every inch of him into her. She heard herself make a sound, a long low moan, as he filled her to her inmost parts. He rose up and took her breasts in his hands, and he rode her with deep strokes. She couldn't move her legs or her arms, only her hips, which she lifted to meet his thrusts. She heard the wet sounds of their copulating and it aroused her even more. Malcolm seemed lost inside her. His hands held her breasts in a firm grip and his head was back, his lips parted, his eyes closed as he fucked her. He was a god to her now, a god of sex and sin. If he could have fucked her forever, she would let him. In hell where the sins of lust were punished, they said the lascivious damned tore each other apart with their desires, and the rent and bleeding pieces still found ways to meet and mate with each other. How was that hell, she wondered? These theologians had never met Malcolm.

The frenzy gripped her, gripped her around the hips and waist. She needed release and it was driving her mad not to have it. Mona rocked her hips faster, lifted and lifted them.

"Easy, love," Malcolm said, but it was too late. She was past all reason. Wild, she bucked as best as she could beneath him with her ankles and wrists bound to the bed. She bucked and writhed, writhed and begged. But Malcolm held back, fucking her with restraint, as if striking her a hundred times with a riding crop wasn't enough torture for her. Not near enough.

This was the worst torture of them all. She had to come. She had to. No question, no hope, no surrender. She needed him to slam his cock into her a thousand times, but he could not be persuaded. He made her suffering even worse when he plucked at her nipples again. He pinched one, then the other, then back and forth. He was giving her gentle foreplay, when what her sex needed was brutal pounding.

"Are you forgetting something?" he asked. That smile again, that evil devil's grin.

She'd forgotten to count.

One hundred strikes. One hundred strokes. She'd forgotten she was supposed to count his thrusts the ways she'd counted the cropping.

"One hundred," she said when Malcolm thrust into her the very next time.

"Now she remembers," he said, still smiling.

He thrust again, harder, and she contracted inside painfully.

"Ninety-nine."

Malcolm pumped his hips again. These were vicious, sharp thrusts, as punishing as they were pleasurable. She could barely recognize her own voice as she counted them. Ninety-eight, ninety-seven…

"By the way, darling, if you come before one hundred, you'll see a side of me you won't like very much."

Ninety-one. Ninety.

The counting kept her from climaxing. She couldn't do both at the same time. The pressure built. The muscles all along the backs of her thighs were so taut she thought they'd snap any moment. And still she lifted her hips into each thrust, not merely receiving his prick but grasping for it with her sex, taking it as it took her.

Eighty-one. Eighty.

To make it even more miserable, Malcolm continued fondling her breasts, pinching her nipples with each number she called out. Her breasts were so swollen from his attentions, they felt twice their normal size.

Seventy-one. Seventy.

She would have given anything to have her ankles free so she could move her legs. She wanted to spread more for him so he could pound her right into the base of her stomach. The very thought of it made her inner muscles twitch.

Sixty-one. Sixty.

Her throat hurt from breathing so hard. She could still taste the salt of his sperm in her mouth.

Fifty-one. Fifty.

Mona pulled on the bonds that held her wrists fast to the bed, anything to relieve some of the excruciating tension in her body. But nothing helped. She was wound tighter than a clock.

Forty-one. Forty.

Malcolm was fucking her harder now. She knew he had to be as desperate to come as she was. Her breasts bounced as he pumped into her cunt.

Thirty-one. Thirty.

He slapped her breasts lightly, reigniting the red pain of the welts. A sound briefly interrupted the counting, part scream and part sob.

Twenty-one. Twenty.

She couldn't take anymore. It was too much. Her head swam and her eyes saw nothing even when open. Her sex throbbed and she could barely speak or breathe or move.

Eleven. Ten.

At last he gave her the thrusts she needed. Full body

thrusts. The soft linen of his shirt grazed her nipples. The stiff shaft grazed her painfully swollen clitoris. She didn't speak the numbers anymore, she gasped them. The bed rocked underneath her and Malcolm was all over her, sucking her and licking her and biting her and fucking and fucking and fucking her.

Two.

One.

The dam burst inside her. With a cry that surely someone heard out on the streets, she came at last, heels dug into the mattress, hips off the bed, and her sex clenching and clutching wildly all around Malcolm's cock. He was coming into her, spurts and spurts of semen glazing her inner walls. Her entire body shuddered and spasmed as she was over-whelmed with the paroxysms of her climax. It went on forever, forever, and even longer than forever…

Then it was done.

Malcolm lay atop her, barely moving, though she felt a few last gasps of fluid spurting inside her. She was spent. She had never been more spent. He'd taken everything out of her. She had nothing left—no mind, no will, no energy.

"Was that enough for you?" Malcolm asked as he nuzzled her ear, kissed her neck.

Already her sex stirred back to life at the sensual tone of his voice, the kisses, the bite of his teeth on her ear.

"No," she said.

"More?"

"More," she begged. "More and more and more." He started to move again, to fuck her again, to fill her again and with each stroke she said that word. More. It was her only want. Her only need.

More.

And more was exactly what he gave her.

VII: DORA AND THE MINOTAUR

*T*he welts took nearly a month to heal. Mona wondered if Malcolm had timed his evening with the crop to coincide with the coming of cold weather. Whatever the cause, she was glad for the chill in the air to give her a reason to keep her body well-covered as she healed from the crop and its hundred kisses.

In the days after that night, she could barely remember the events without trembling and hiding herself in her office until she'd gotten hold of herself again. How had he done it? Trained her so quickly to crave pain? And she'd asked him permission to love him? What had possessed her to ask him about his children?

Possessed her. That was it. She felt like he'd gotten into her soul somehow, into her mind, and had taken control of her body and her brain. The thoughts she had of him kept her up at night—sometimes weeping with shame, more often burning with longing. Not a day passed she didn't make herself come once or twice. One day, four times when she became fixated on the specific memory of her lips on his boot buttons, how she'd worshiped him on her hands and knees, how she'd opened her holes up to him in an offering that he'd accepted with a vicious lash of his crop. No man had ever made her feel so much as Malcolm did. Pain didn't cancel out the pleasure—it doubled it, trebled it. With other lovers she'd felt pleasure and lust. With Malcolm she felt pleasure and lust, but also pain and fear, love and hate. It was the most potent of alchemies. She would have sold herself to him every night of her life for another taste of those boot buttons.

Mona didn't know what to do with herself while she waited for Malcolm's return. She tried focusing on her work. Malcolm had left her a pen and ink drawing by German-American cartoonist Lyonel Feinenger as payment for the night with the crop, and she liked it so much she knew she wouldn't sell it to pay off her debt unless she absolutely had to. The drawing was of two ghosts carrying their own urns while a tall and skinny black cat stared wide-eyed at the pair of silly spirits.

A handful of gallery events had generated a little income for The Red, but the debt still loomed, growing larger with interest every day. She treated it like she treated fantasies of Malcolm, chasing them from her mind whenever they reared their heads.

Still…she thought of him.

Mona wanted to believe Malcolm had some feelings for her. Feelings other than simple lust or desire. He never left until she fell asleep, and she often fell asleep with him inside of her, his ardor for her body far greater than her stamina. She'd asked him the night with the crop why he came to her so infrequently and he'd said their encounters were taxing, that it took him time to recover. She found that difficult to believe. A man with his libido worn out for a month or two from one night of sex? Impossible. No, he must have a wife waiting for him in England. She'd worked up the courage to ask him about his children, but she couldn't stomach mentioning a wife. Though if his children were grown as he said, why wouldn't he leave his wife? If he even had a wife? Was she the source of all his money? Is that why he stayed with her? Or was he divorced, and something else took him back to England for weeks on end? Grandchildren? She'd guessed his age at forty. If he were older—forty-five perhaps —it wouldn't be unreasonable at all for him to have a grand-child or two if he had married in his early twenties and his children had too. She shouldn't think about such things, about his home life, about what he did when he wasn't with her. A girl could go crazy letting her mind run along that rabbit trail. Her brain felt like a horse on a carousel, always moving but going nowhere.

October turned to November, and the orange and red leaves turned brown and then fell to the sidewalk where they made their final transformation to sooty black. The crisp air turned cold. This would be her first holiday season without her mother. Mona had friends, but she'd seen little of them since Malcolm came into her life. She cried off dinners and movies, pleading poverty and exhaustion. She didn't want her friends asking her what was going on. In a weak moment she might tell them, and since meeting Malcolm she'd had nothing but weak moments. She tried to put herself in her friends' shoes. What would she say if her college roommate Natasha called and said she'd sold her body to a man—a man with no last name, a man who didn't use condoms, a man who had no qualms about fucking other women in front of her or bringing other men to their sessions to fondle and finger her? No, Mona couldn't tell anyone. They might try to talk her out of doing it, and that was the last thing she wanted. She could either see Malcolm or she could see reason, and Malcolm was a finer sight than anything as dull as reason.

November turned to December.

Mona's body had healed completely, no marks left at all. It shamed her how much she missed them when they were gone. She'd started sleeping in the bed in the gallery's back room. First she slept there only one night a week. Then two. Now she slept there almost every night, little Tou-Tou on the pillow that should have been Malcolm's. She'd rise early, go home to shower and change clothes, and then return to the gallery. If she'd had a full bathroom at The Red, she would have lived there. In the brass bed, even alone, she felt closer to Malcolm. Even after washing and replacing the sheets, she could still smell the faint cedar and cigar smoke scent of him when she laid on the pillow at night. She hoped it would never fade. Any ideas she had about ever selling the bed disappeared. As long as she lived she would keep the bed she'd shared with Malcolm. She wanted to conceive a child in it, his child. It's what her mother had done after all—gone to bed with a strange man she met at a party for the sole reason of having a child on her own. Maybe he would allow that as long as she promised never to trouble him for money or support. It was what her mother would have wanted Mona to do. Maybe Mona could have convinced herself to follow through on this plan and abandon her birth control except it was nearing Christmas. This was the time of year when she wished the hardest she knew who her father was and where he was. With her mother gone, she had no family at all with whom to spend the holiday. She wasn't sure she could do that to her child. The dream would have to have to stay a dream. It wasn't as if she had the money to raise a child on her own anyway. Admit it, she told herself, you want him to love you.

She admitted it, but only to herself.

The week before Christmas, the gallery phone rang after

hours. She picked it up and was pleased to hear Sebastian's voice on the line.

"How have you been?" he asked. "Do you have more Degas sketches to show me?"

"None, I'm afraid," she said with a laugh. "You'd be my first phone call if I did."

"There's a Degas exhibit this month. Have you seen it?"

"I haven't, no. Worth the trip?"

"How could you ask me such a thing? I'd walk across a desert with no water for a Degas exhibit and this one is only a cab ride uptown. Come with me. I'll tell you all of the master's secrets. You can see the final result of that sketch you have. It's on exhibit. You won't regret it."

"Now where have I heard that before?"

Oh yes, from Malcolm.

Hungry for company, Mona agreed to meet him at the exhibit. But only to meet him. She didn't want him thinking it was a date, even if it sort of was. She was too far gone in whatever this was with Malcolm to get romantically entangled with anyone else. But still, Sebastian was terribly handsome with his curling dark hair, warm brown skin, and vibrant eyes. And he knew everything there was to know about Degas—his art, his life. Sebastian's enthusiasm was infectious. She would have to see about getting a whole display of Degas sketches at The Red. When it was time to part, she kissed Sebastian on the lips—a quick small kiss, but more than she'd intended. As he put her in a cab to send her home, she realized she'd gone two whole hours without thinking of Malcolm. A small victory, but one she'd desperately needed on a cold gray Saturday in a lonely December.

As usual, she went to the gallery instead of her apartment. She pretended she was there solely to check Tou-Tou's food and water, but she knew what she wanted was to work so late she could justify, yet again, sleeping in the brass bed in

the back room. When she walked into her office, she found a
book and a glass of red wine waiting on her desk.

Malcolm was back.

Mona could hardly catch her breath as she walked to her
desk and sat down in the ancient swivel chair that needed
oiling. She looked at the wine first. A white card sat propped
up on the glass stem. On it in bold male handwriting were
two words.

Drink me.

If he left the wine for her to drink, that meant he
intended to have her tonight. She wondered vaguely if he
was watching her and knew she'd gone out with Sebastian. Is
that why he wanted her tonight? Usually he gave her a day's
warning. If he wanted her to drink it now, though…

And why the wine? One glass wouldn't intoxicate her. At
most it would relax her. But for what purpose, what plan?
He'd beaten her with a riding crop last time without this sort
of preparation. She couldn't begin to guess why he needed
her to drink. Carte blanche, she reminded herself. She'd
given him carte blanche. If she needed to drink a little before
whatever it was he had planned for her, she would do it.

She sipped at it gingerly. It was unlike any red she'd had,
but once she discovered its subtle sweetness, she drank
deeper and faster. On her empty stomach, the wine went to
her head quickly. However, although red wine had a depres-
sive effect, it did nothing to settle the tempest in her heart or
quiet the storm in her blood.

She turned her attention to the book. A slim volume of
blue, with "Picasso" printed on the spine. So tonight was to
be surreal in some way? Her vision was already beginning to
blur thanks to the potent red wine. Potent and delicious. She
couldn't get enough of it. She drank every drop of the wine
before setting the empty glass on the desk and opening the
book to the page marked with her red velvet choker.

Mona blinked when she saw the painting. Then she giggled. Oh, Malcolm. The painting was called *Dora and the Minotaur*. It was a large, brightly colored work. A naked woman lay on her back as a pale Minotaur—a creature with a bull's head and a man's body—mounted her. Dora Maar, according to the book, had been Picasso's muse and mistress. And he often painted the Minotaur as a symbol of himself. From what she knew of Picasso's personality and libido, he had chosen his avatar well.

So it was to be role play again? She imagined Malcolm wearing a leather mask, with horns on his head and a bull's large sloped eyes. A laughable idea. She wouldn't put it past him at all. She recalled the satyr's role he'd played so well, the hairy leggings that had felt so warm and real, the pointed ears. Well, she would play along. Where Malcolm was concerned she was up for anything. She swayed a little on her feet as she rose from her desk. Malcolm was no doubt already waiting for her in their back room.

As she walked to the door, another memory stirred. Hadn't Malcolm said something about how she would hate him next time? He had, yes. The night with the riding crop kisses, he'd given her permission to love him since next time they met she would hate him. Now that was laughable, utterly laughable. She couldn't hate Malcolm. Another mind game. She was growing fond of them.

Mona slowly opened the back room door. It was dark inside. Completely dark. The sun had set and no light shown through the skylight. No light at all. Strange. There should have been some ambient light in the room from the street lamps and the moon. But no, the room was pitch black. The door shut behind her and she leaned her back against it, afraid of taking another step in the dark lest she trip and fall.

"Malcolm?"

He didn't answer her call.

Something else was off. Usually the room smelled of nothing but clean dust, the scent of old books, old theaters, old paint. After a night with Malcolm it smelled of cigar smoke and sex. But now it smelled like an animal had been in here. A large animal. Was that the wine's doing? A breeze blew past her, warm like a sea breeze. Her nose twitched. There was that scent again. A kind of animal musk. The smell troubled her nose. It didn't belong in here. She fumbled for the doorknob behind her and felt a string tied to it. She followed the string with her fingers and found it extended far into the room. Now she understood the darkness—she was to follow the string where it led. There was an old myth about the labyrinth, a thread to guide a girl... Who was the girl, again? Ariadne? She'd been out of school too long to say for certain. But she knew the string was to guide her through the labyrinth. She took a steadying breath and stepped forward, thread in hand. Malcolm certainly went all out for these assignations. No wonder two months could pass between their liaisons. It would take anyone that long to put these sorts of scenes together. Perhaps he'd majored in theater at university.

She giggled a little drunkenly at the thought. Oh no, not laughing already. It would likely hurt Malcolm's feelings if she laughed at this production of his. She must be very solemn. Following the string in her hand, Mona felt herself walking toward the center of the back room. She sensed walls on either side of her. Malcolm had constructed a whole set for tonight. How flattering it was he went to so much trouble when she would have met him in a seedy motel had he asked it of her. Of course he went to all this trouble to please himself, not her, but she couldn't deny she enjoyed that he took their assignations so seriously.

Ahead of her she caught a glimpse of light, red and flickering. The thread led her to turn a corner and she saw a fat white candle alight on the floor in the middle of a blank hall-way. She picked up the candle in its holder and raised it. The candle illuminated only the few feet around her, and she saw nothing ahead but the white thread she held. The walls on either side of her were narrow. They looked and felt like stone to her. But that was highly unlikely. It wouldn't take long to build a maze out of large sheets of plywood, but a stone maze would take weeks. He was either a very good set designer or she had been drugged.

Considering how light she felt, how fluttery and faint, she figured it was the latter. Malcolm had spiked the wine with some drug or other, one that made her very susceptible to the power of suggestion and also made her care not one whit that he'd drugged her.

Tomorrow, however, she'd be furious at him.

For now, she followed the thread. At the end of the hall she met another corridor. The string told her to go right, but she was more curious to see what was left. She turned her head and saw an enormous shadow move at the end of the hall. She jumped back with a gasp, nearly dropping the candle.

The shadow disappeared into the darkness. It had seemed far too tall, too wide to be human. Was this the Minotaur?

No. Not possible. Shapes were distorted when thrown into shadow, she reminded herself. The drugs had done this to her mind. Surely it was nothing. Her eyes were playing games with her too.

Mona glanced behind her and narrowed her eyes. Nothing. She saw nothing. But she heard something.

A growl.

A deep, low, animal growl, like a large dog or wolf.

"Malcolm?" she called out again. It made her feel safer to say his name.

He made no reply, no answer at all.

But he wouldn't, would he? Not until the game was over.

She chided herself for giving into fear. This was nothing but a Halloween haunted house. That's all. He'd set up a painted plywood maze in the large back room while she was out at the Degas exhibit. He'd covered the skylight. He'd put a string on the doorknob and when she found her way to the end of it, she would find Malcolm, naked, reclining on the bed and wearing a silly bull's mask. He'd throw her onto the bed, probably put her on her hands and knees, and then he'd mount her from behind like a bull on a cow. That's all. No reason for her to feel such fear. She blamed the wine for her overreaction—the wine, and whatever Malcolm had put into it.

Carefully she started forward again. The candle flame sent dancing shadows everywhere and they did nothing to help steady her head or clear her vision. She focused on the white thread in her hand. This was her life line. It would take her to Malcolm or take her back out again. Nothing bad would happen as long as she had this candle and this silk thread in her hands.

She came to a corner and turned. At the intersection where one hall met the other, she saw a hooded person, cloaked and wearing a cowl. Mona screamed and threw herself back against the wall. The figure was gone. She hadn't seen where it had come from or where it had disappeared, but disappeared it had. She thought it had worn red.

Distant music echoed through the halls.

It wasn't like the sprightly flute music of the nymphs and the satyr. She heard low rumbling drums. Chanting. She couldn't make out any of the words of the chant, but the voices sounded female. She was certain the creature in the red cloak had been male. She'd only seen it for a split second, but its bulk had filled every inch of the corridor. Its shoulders were twice as broad as hers, its height towering. Something told her it hadn't seen her.

"It."

The Minotaur.

Calm down, she told herself. The shadowy figure wasn't an "it." The "Minotaur" was either Malcolm in a costume or one of his many compatriots. He seemed to have a bevy of play partners for his erotic adventures. Any one of them could have donned a cloak to frighten her, that was all.

She followed the cord a few more steps and the music grew louder. She was nearing the end. The thread led her through another turn in the maze and there she smelled that animal scent again. It was strong in her nostrils and strangely pleasant. A smell like raw nature, like a horse might smell after a long dusty trail ride.

For all her foreboding, Mona couldn't deny she was excited, even a little aroused. Malcolm was somewhere in this maze, and he wanted her to find him. Soon she would be safe in his arms, his cock lodged inside her right where it belonged. Once she found him, she would be fine. It was only a game, after all. Only a game of cat and mouse. She was the mouse, of course. She must be ready for Malcolm's pounce.

Step by dreadful step, Mona made her way through the maze. Rationally, she knew she'd only gone about forty feet at most. Yet it felt like a mile for all the twists and turns, all the darkness, and the surreality of it all. The music grew louder still—if it could be called music, this odd atonal chant. Malcolm was using it to scare her. She refused to let it work on her like that. She wasn't a child to be frightened by costumes and lighting effects.

A thought occurred to Mona out of nowhere, a thought and a question: Did her mother have this in mind when she'd told Mona to do anything to save the gallery?

Likely not.

Mona pressed on. A breeze gusted through the corridor and blew out her candle. She was frightened at first, but she found another source of light at the end of the hall. She set the candle down and continued on, toward the flickering red light dancing on the wall. At the end of that hall she turned right and found herself at the mouth of a cave. Ten paces ahead a small wood fire burned in the center of a ring of stones. She saw more figures in cloaks around the fire and behind them a massive boulder, wide as a car, tall as a man. Mona's head spun again, her eyes watered. What the hell had Malcolm put in her drink? A hallucinogenic? Dazed by the chanting, by the fire, by the drug in her blood, Mona stepped forward out of the cave mouth. The bowed heads of the cloaked figures raised and she saw they were women with sooty black painted across their eyes and temples like a bandit's mask. She wanted to scream, but everything went black.

When she came to, she lay on the ground by the fire. It felt like warm and real earth to her, not the hardwood floor of the back room. The rational part of her brain unaffected by the drug knew she'd been transported somewhere after fainting. She wasn't in the back room. That had been misdirection. She'd passed out—probably the drug's doing—and she'd been driven into the woods where the scene would continue in the open. She saw the twinkling of stars overhead. A ring of trees, large and ancient. Oaks, perhaps? And she smelled wild grass, rich dark dirt, fresh air.

But that made no sense either. She was warm, almost hot. Earlier, she'd had to wear a coat to the exhibit because of the chilly winter weather.

The coven of cloaked women stirred silently when Mona opened her eyes. They looked at each and nodded. Mona counted six of them, all of indeterminate age behind their sooty masks and hoods. They seemed to be playing the role of ancient Greek priestesses in this pantomime, and they certainly looked the part with their olive-toned complexions and black braids draped over their shoulders. At once, all six of them reached for her on the ground and lifted her bodily into the air, turning her to stand on her feet. They took the pins from her hair and let it fall in red waves around her shoulders. Fingers sought and found the buttons to Mona's black blouse, the zipper to her red skirt, the hooks to the stockings she'd worn to the Degas exhibit in case she changed her mind about going to bed with Sebastian. It seemed they managed to strip her naked without touching her skin. Mona had anticipated being naked tonight, so she didn't struggle. When they were done, Mona stood amid the women, her eyes to the ground. It felt so real, looked and smelled so real. She pawed at the dirt with her toe and it moved like soft earth, not dirt sprinkled across a finished floor. They'd taken her somewhere—they'd had to have. Hadn't they? She heard an owl in the distance. A sound effect, a hallucination...or something else?

One woman seemed to be the leader, the eldest. By the firelight Mona could see her hands were those of an elderly woman. The high priestess? Whoever she was, she was holding a stone knife. Mona flinched from the sight of it flickering red in the firelight. She pulled back and away from it, but the cloaked women behind her grabbed her and held her in place, trapping her arms behind her back. The woman raised her hands. Her left was empty, but in her right she held aloft the stone knife. Without warning, she pricked at the center of her own left palm with the knife. Blood bubbled up from the wound. The knife disappeared into the folds of the cloak and the high priestess stepped toward Mona. She touched the blood in her palm delicately, brought her red fingers to Mona's face and dabbed the blood across her eyelids and temples, giving Mona the same markings as the women, only in red, not black.

Mona fainted again—from the shock of the blood or from the drug, she didn't know. When she woke again from the brief faint, the women were dragging her toward the boulder. One side of the stone was curved and smooth, as if a thousand years of water had worn off its rough edges. Iron spikes had been driven deep into the sides of the boulder, and from them hung iron chains. The women lifted Mona off her feet. They pressed her back into the stone and held her down by her arms and legs. The high priestess bound her wrists to the boulder with the iron chains and drew another chain across her stomach, leaving only her legs free. The cloaked women released her all at once and formed a straight line facing her. Even without their hands, Mona stayed in place, the chains holding her fast to the boulder. Struggling proved useless and did nothing but abrade her back against the stone. Due to the irregular shape of the boulder, Mona's body curved in an obscene arch, her breasts lifted high and her hips tilted forward.

All at once the women moved. The six of them parted down the center, revealing the red-cloaked figure behind them, the figure she'd seen in the maze.

It towered over the women, dwarfing them by several feet. Mona could not see its face hidden within the folds of the cloak, but she knew it stared at her. She wanted to scream but her voice was gone. She would faint again any moment. This time, she hoped she wouldn't come to until morning.

But she didn't faint. The figure stepped forward and she could hear its animal breathing now. Not a wolf or a bear or a dog, but certainly something large and lethal. She feared it. No amount of telling herself her senses were distorted by a drug in her drink could convince her not to fear this beast, the Minotaur.

The chanting of the women began again. Not Latin. Greek, perhaps? Some far more ancient language?

The Minotaur stepped closer. This couldn't be Malcolm, could it? Malcolm was tall, but not nearly this gargantuan. No human man was this tall, this broad, this massive.

It stepped closer yet, so close she felt the heat radiating from it. Against the stone she shook and shivered. A hand extended—a human hand, thank God—from within the red cloak. It was huge, this hand, muscular and veined like Malcolm's, but even larger. The hand touched her face gently, so gently. It stroked her quivering lips and dabbed at the tears on her cheek. The Minotaur seemed to be trying to soothe her and calm her. He—no longer "it," for there was a man in there, no matter how distorted—caressed her hair, the line of her jaw, her ears. Her heart rate slowed. Her eyes fluttered. What was he doing to her? Hypnotizing her? She felt calmer than she ever had in her life. It was like a trance, like a waking sleep. Her body went slack against the boulder as if it were the softest of beds, not the hardest of stones. The man in the red cloak extended his other hand. He slid it behind her, cradling her head in his massive palm to protect it from the hard unforgiving rock she lay chained against.

"Malcolm?" she whispered, hoping he would respond in some way, letting her know that somehow this was him even if the drug he'd given her had turned him into this funhouse mirror version of himself, so much larger than any normal man. Though he said nothing and did nothing to reveal himself, she sensed it was Malcolm. Something in the way his fingers touched her face told her it was him. She was not afraid anymore. They were playing at human sacrifice tonight, he the beast and she the offering. He the Minotaur, and she Dora. It was only another game.

The man stepped so close his cloak brushed her naked skin. She shivered at the contact, the soft prickle of the velvet on her bare legs, a sensation delicious to her heightened senses. As he positioned himself between her open thighs, she searched out any sign of his face within the hood of the cloak, but the cowl and the darkness obscured his features from her. Somehow, the hidden face was far more unsettling than the leather bull mask she'd pictured.

The enormous hand touching her face moved to her right breast. The Minotaur took the nipple in his fingers and pinched it, then pulled lightly on it. Yes, it was Malcolm, or some version of him. It had to be. This was how he touched her, possessively, without warning or apology. Her breast seemed so small in the massive hand that fondled it. She was grateful for the hand behind her head as she squirmed in her chains. He fondled her other breast next, groping it, squeezing and pawing at it. The rough treatment aroused her though she didn't want it to. She extended a leg into the folds of his cloak and felt a rock hard male thigh. She raised her other leg and found another thigh. It was warm within his cloak. His skin was shockingly hot to the touch and in the cool night air she craved that heat. The man grunted as she wrapped her legs around his waist, and his hot breath blew over her face. The hand on her breast slipped between her legs. He probed with his fingers, seeking her wetness and finding it. He pushed his thumb and forefinger inside her. She moaned like an animal when he spread his fingers apart at the opening of her body, then did it again deeper. He was preparing her to receive his cock. She felt the organ now, massive as the rest of him. It pressed against her inner thigh, hotter even than the rest of his body, dripping fluid and hard as the stone behind her. She craved it terribly, even though its exaggerated size scared her.

He removed his hand and notched the tip of the organ at

the slit of her vulva. It was too big to fit. It would tear her open if she took it. She shrank from it, but there was nowhere to hide or run. The man lowered his cloaked head to her chest and flicked his tongue across her nipple. It felt strange, not like Malcolm's tongue or mouth on her. It was oddly cold, but not unpleasantly so. Over and over again he lapped at her nipple and licked the entire breast with long strokes. With each flick and lick of the tongue, the man's massive member eased a little deeper into her hole. Mona rocked her hips to take even more of it. The Minotaur grunted again, an inhuman sound that would have scared her had she not been so lost in the pleasure of the penetration. Deep vaginal muscles groaned in protest as his great organ split her apart, pushing the walls open as it burrowed further into her. With her legs fastened tight around him, she anchored herself and worked her hips up and down. The pleasure was unholy. She went wild with it. He rose up and thrust into her. She cried out as he filled her completely, more completely than she'd ever been filled. She couldn't bear it. She had to have it out of her. A spurt of his seed hit her cervix and she orgasmed suddenly from the incredible force and heat of it. He thrust again and the slick seed inside her eased his passage. The enormous organ moved far more easily inside her now that he'd ejaculated. And yet it seemed the fierce coupling had only begun.

His thrusts were slow and deliberate. He pulled out to the tip and entered her by inches. He was close to her, so close that she could raise her head from the stone and nuzzle it against his chest if she could somehow part the folds of the cloak. The coven of women still chanted though Mona barely heard it. The man said nothing. They copulated in total silence but for their breathing. Her thighs were damp and she felt more fluid dripping down the rock under her hips. Minutes passed. He moved faster inside her but not fast

enough to bring her to a second orgasm. She sensed something building, something more than her own climax. The
chanting grew louder, his thrusts harder and deeper. Even
chained to the rock, Mona felt her body floating, weightless,
unmoored. Again the colossal hand found her breasts and
fondled them, pulling on the hardened points, squeezing
them mercilessly. The hand was perfect in all ways but for its
freakish size, and she couldn't stop herself from arching
against the huge palm. She was torn between her desire for
his rough caresses and her need to shrink from this cloaked
creature, run from it, hide. But where could she go? Even if
she weren't chained to the rock, the cock inside her speared
her to the boulder as completely as an iron stake through her
body.

The Minotaur—the man, Malcolm, whatever or whoever
he was—lifted her back off the boulder and slipped his arm
under her. They were sealed together at the loins. Another
spurt of seed filled her and she orgasmed again. Only with
Malcolm had she ever been able to feel a man coming inside
her. It should be over now. No man could come twice inside
a woman and continue to fuck her afterwards. It was unnat-
ural. It wasn't possible. Yet he continued to thrust into her
hole. Her sex felt like an open wound, the tissue wet and raw
and pried apart.

She needed it to stop.

She never wanted it to end.

He took his hand out from behind her head and grasped
her thigh. The other hand held the other thigh. He jerked her
hips toward him, impaling her on him as he impaled himself
into her. The chanting grew ever louder until it was all she
could hear. It was louder than her breathing, louder than his,
louder than their coupling, louder than her own cries as he
rode her toward a final climax. She thrashed on the rock,
turned her head and buried it against her arm, screamed as

muscles inside her spread, twisted and rearranged themselves to accommodate that inhuman organ thrusting inside of her.

Would it ever end? Yes, it had to. She felt it nearing its end, speeding toward the final cataclysm. She tried to hasten the end with wild gyrations, and the cloaked man responded with faster thrusts. It was a primal union of bodies. There was nothing left of Mona—not her name, her past, her life in the outside world. There was no outside world. There was the joining of their bodies, the wetness, the rock behind her and the cloak shielding her and nothing else. The Minotaur penetrated every part of that devouring orifice. It was coming. She could feel it. It was coming. Almost there. It was coming. The final spasm of union. It was coming. The closing of the wound. It was coming. The sacrifice that brought them together. It was coming. It was coming. The man pounded into her depths. She looked up at the night sky and saw all the stars turn red.

It was coming.

The man pulled back his hood and Mona screamed.

"It's me, darling," Malcolm said into her ear. "It's only me."

Mona found herself in the bed in the back room, Malcolm, naked on top of her, inside of her, moving within her. Mona's orgasm shook her down to her core, her cervix contracting wildly, painfully almost, even as she screamed again in her terror.

The Minotaur—the cloaked figure who was but was not Malcolm—was gone. So were the fire and the priestesses and the chanting and the chains around her wrists and stomach and the bolder against her back. In their place there was nothing but a candle burning on a stool, paintings of women around and about the bed, the sounds of the street, and Malcolm's own weight holding her down onto the bed.

She pushed him off her and sat back against the headboard, semen pouring out of her. Malcolm knelt in front of her, an ironic smile on his face.

"Did I give you a little fright?" he teased.

"A little fright? You drugged me."

"Never. It was nothing more than pomegranate wine. Then again, pomegranates do have very special powers."

"That was not just wine. What I saw—"

"You saw what I wanted you to see as always. When you drink it, it opens the mind."

Her heart raced like she was still chained to the boulder. Her hands shook, her entire body shook.

"I warned you I like to play games," he said. "I warned you that next time, you would hate me."

"I do hate you."

"It'll pass." He shrugged, sent her a kiss and a wink. "It always does."

"Get out," she said.

"If you insist. I wasn't quite finished with you. But no harm, no foul," Malcolm said, waving a hand dismissively. He climbed off the bed and quickly dressed in his three-piece suit. "Next time we'll end on a better note."

"No next time. I don't want you to ever come back."

"I'm afraid we had an agreement, did we not? You recall this?" He pulled a crisp white rectangle of paper from his inner breast pocket. He showed her one side—white and blank—and the other side, also white and blank. "You agreed to do anything."

"You drugged me. You made me hallucinate."

"I didn't, actually…but even if I did, that would fall under the umbrella of 'anything,' wouldn't you agree?"

Mona snatched the card from his hand and ripped it into pieces. She sent them scattering all over the bed.

"Get out. Never come back."

"You don't mean it."

She pulled away from him, turned her back on him, and wouldn't look at him.

"You're a monster," she said, a sob rising in her throat.

"It was only pretend. I warned you…"

He had warned her she wouldn't know fantasy from reality. He had, but this was different. Fantasy and reality were one thing, but Malcolm had made her question her very sanity.

"Get away from me. Now."

He slammed the door so loudly she jumped. The candle blew out, and the room went dark but for the skylight.

Only pretend, he'd said.

Pretend? No one's imagination was that good, certainly not hers. He had drugged her. She knew he'd drugged her. The violation of her trust was unforgivable.

Mona dressed in yesterday's clothes and checked the time —it was nearly dawn. Hours had passed since she'd drunk the wine he'd left for her by the book. She would have to hurry. She didn't want the drugs leaving her system before she could be tested for them. Hospital emergency wards were slow, but if she left now, she might make it back before opening the gallery at ten. Not that it mattered much. The gallery would go under without Malcolm's financial support. But she would rather watch barbarian hordes tear it down brick by brick than allow Malcolm to touch one hair on her head ever again. No man was allowed to drug her. She knew he liked to play games, but this was too far. Whatever his endgame was, she wanted no part of it.

She gathered the pieces of the white card off the bed and tossed them into the trash in her office.

The game was over.

VIII: THE BLEEDING MAN

*P*omegranate wine and nothing else.

No opium, no LSD, no mushrooms, nothing.

Mona couldn't believe it. A few days after her panicked trip to a doctor, she got the call with her test results. There had been no drugs in her system, none at all. Only alcohol, and not even enough of it to make a dent in her senses.

She thanked the nurse who called. The woman sounded concerned, suggested Mona talk to a police officer if she believed someone had tried to drug her. Or perhaps a therapist if her drinking was causing her to black out.

Mona drank little, and when she did it was rarely enough to get drunk. And what would she tell the police if she did call them? She'd agreed to whore herself to a man without a last name who paid her in artwork? That he'd given her a glass of pomegranate wine full of an untraceable hallucinogenic and somehow he'd made her believe she was chained to a boulder in a sacred forest being sexually sacrificed to a cloaked and hooded Minotaur so much larger than any man?

She'd be in a mental hospital by lunch.

A week after that night, Mona went hunting and tracked

down pomegranate wine in a specialty liquor store. Alone at her apartment, she drank a glass of it on an empty stomach. It was delicious, yes, sweet and tart, but it did nothing but give her the typical buzz any glass of red wine would. Malcolm had claimed pomegranates had special properties, but when she researched the fruit she found nowhere that claimed it could cause hallucinations, even when fermented.

One line about pomegranates did catch her eye, however. The Greeks called it "the fruit of the dead," and was once believed to have come from the veins of the Greek god Adonis. Pomegranate, the only fruit that grew in Hades. Myth and legend. Pomegranate wine would not have made her seen what she had seen, do what she had done, enjoy what she had enjoyed. Something else was at play. But what?

After their fight, Malcolm made no attempts to see her or contact her in any way. She thought he wasn't even going to pay her for their encounter until she came to the gallery three weeks after that bizarre red-cloaked night and found an empty red wine bottle on her desk, the cork pushed back inside the mouth. She took the cork out, not wanting to know what Malcolm had left for her. She turned the bottle over and the white card pieces fluttered out. He'd come here while she was gone, gathered them up and put them into the bottle. What did it mean? Was he trying to tell her again that she'd promised him carte blanche? She remembered their first night together. He'd used her glass water bottle inside her as a dildo, fucking her with it. She'd called it perverse and he'd teased her that it could be worse, he could have used a wine bottle.

That's what the message meant. It could have been worse.

In anger, she gathered every single little scrap of fine white paper in the bottle and dropped it into her wastepaper basket. She could not be bought or cajoled into seeing him again.

It was over.

Underneath the bottle was a linen napkin. She lifted the linen and underneath it was another sketch.

A close-up of a ballerina's hand, she knew on sight it was a Degas. A beautiful sketch beautifully done. Sebastian would be overjoyed to see it—and her. Oh, he'd be overjoyed to see her again. He'd phoned her twice since they'd gone to the exhibit, and she'd put him off with vague excuses about not feeling well. He'd been sympathetic, if disappointed. She wondered why she told him no. She'd been furious at Malcolm because she'd been certain he'd drugged her. Then she'd learned he likely hadn't, and she was desperate to find another reason to stay angry at him. He hadn't raped her. She'd been a willing participant and had agreed to let him do whatever he wanted to her as long as she wasn't physically harmed. And he hadn't harmed her physically, not unless she counted have an aching back and swollen vulva the morning after. She told herself he'd made her distrust her own senses, made her question reality, made her think impossible things could and did happen, and that was unforgivable. Because impossible things didn't happen and if they did they wouldn't be impossible. If she hadn't been drugged, then the maze had been real—and so had the clearing in the woods, the coven of priestesses and the horror of the Minotaur who'd copulated with her. She had no proof he'd drugged her. No proof the maze wasn't real. What was she to believe? That it had happened as she remembered it? No, she refused to believe it. She'd be on the road to madness next.

Once she reconciled herself to never knowing the truth, Mona did her best to put that mad night and all the memories of it behind her. During the day she could occupy herself with work and her constant fears over the gallery's imminent closing. But at night she dreamed of Malcolm and the beast he'd become and the enormous cock inside her. She would wake up orgasming, wishing to feel the rock under her back once more. Sometimes she even wept. The need to see Malcolm again and spread her legs for him and be taken by him was so strong it left her breathless, reeling, half-sick and miserable. Every night she'd sneak Tou-Tou into her apartment for the sole reason that she could not stand to be alone at night anymore. She passed New Year's in her bed reading a book and cuddling with Tou-Tou on her chest. The thought of going out and smiling for friends and flirting with strangers made her dizzy. She wanted nothing to do with the world outside her gallery anymore.

Mona couldn't go on like this forever. She refused to. Every day she came into the gallery fearful of finding a message from Malcolm, more fearful she wouldn't. A month passed without him returning to put the red velvet choker into a book of art. Then six weeks. Her resolved started to crumble. She felt it breaking down, heard it cracking. But she stayed adamant—she would not give in and forgive Malcolm.

The Degas sketch of the ballerina's hand waited in a folder in her desk. It felt like a test, somehow. Like Malcolm knew about Sebastian, knew he tempted her.

On a quiet Friday she closed the gallery early and called Sebastian.

"I have something for you," she said.

"The words every man longs to hear from a beautiful woman."

"Can you come see it?" she asked, smiling at his voice, so warm and solid and kind.

"Tell me when."

"Right now," she said. "I'll be at my gallery all evening working in the back room. I'll leave the side door unlocked for you."

"I'm on my way," he said. "Then I'm buying you dinner. I won't take no for an answer. Unless you mean it."

She laughed softly. "I won't say no," she said. She wouldn't say no to anything.

As soon as she hung up the phone a wave of nervousness washed over her. It was late January and she hadn't let herself be intimate with any man except Malcolm since June. Malcolm had consumed her life for far too long. She'd stopped going out, stopped dating, stopping seeing her female friends out of fear they'd judge her for Malcolm. She didn't want to bear their judgment, especially knowing they would have done the same if they only saw him, spent one night with him.

She had to get over Malcolm any way she could. Any way at all.

When Sebastian knocked softly on the door to the back room, she opened it.

She was naked.

He stared at her a long tense moment, only stared. He was handsome as ever. Brown eyes, not black. Brown hair, not black. Tan skin, not pale. He wore a normal suit, not a three-piece—tailored gray trousers, black and gray tie, white shirt and jacket—and he wore it well.

All at once he moved, without warning, taking her in his arms and kissing her. His tongue pushed into her mouth the second she opened it to him. His hands were all over her back and bottom and shoulders. He kissed her so hard he nearly bent her backwards. He turned her and pushed her back to the door and groped her breasts. He dropped his head to her nipple and drew it deep into his mouth, so deep it almost hurt, and she sighed because this was what she'd missed, this was what she craved. Already she was wet, already she wanted him inside her. She told him as much and he looked up at her with surprise. Then he had her by the arm, dragging her to the bed. She hadn't expected this sort of intensity from Sebastian, but it pleased her to no end that he could be so commanding, so demanding. The bed was made and he didn't bother to pull the covers back before he pushed her down onto her back by the footboard and climbed on top of her. With his knees he pushed her thighs open while he unzipped his pants and pushed them down his thighs. His penis was hard already and jutting upward out of a thick patch of black hair. She reached for it, needing it, and he pushed her hand aside. She lifted her hips in invitation, and he entered her with a rough stroke. She cried out in relief and joy.

Bliss. The purest bliss. He drove his cock into her with more rough thrusts. It was a thick organ with an upward curve that tickled a tender spot under her navel. He played with her breasts while he fucked her, tugging on the tips, massaging them with his whole hands. Her head lay at the edge of the mattress and each thrust pushed her head further off the bed. She arched her back and the world turned upside down. It was dizzying, being fucked like this, but she relished it. Anything to stop her from thinking of Malcolm. Sebastian didn't fuck like Malcolm. His penis felt different inside her, and whereas Malcolm made soft dirty grunting sounds during sex, Sebastian stayed completely silent. Even his face was silent, no expression as he rode her hard. She raised her head and watched him fucking her. When he saw her looking so intently, he pulled out of her, grabbed her by the arm and yanked her up. Mona let herself be putty in his hands. He could put her in any position, take her any way he wanted. Sebastian placed her on her hands and knees on the bed, and left her there waiting for him while he stripped naked quickly, discarding his clothes all over the floor in his haste to get back inside her. He took her by the hips and entered her again from behind. His hands cupped her breasts and held them while he rode her with long thrusts. He seemed in no hurry to orgasm and she was pleased he was taking his time inside her. He brought his middle fingers to his lips, licked them and then ran the wet fingertips around and over her nipples. Without asking she knew he'd fantasized about doing just this to her—entering her bare, licking his fingers, fondling her nipples... Mona wanted him to do everything he'd fantasized about doing to her and she told him. He laughed softly at her words, grabbed a handful of her bottom, pinched it hard and then slapped it. The sound rang out in the room. A spank, an ass slap, normal sexual fantasies. No nymphs. No slave auction. No riding crop. No maze, no grove, no Minotaur. It was better like this, this normal human sex without Malcolm's bizarre fantasies, without the games he played on her body and her mind. Wasn't it?

Across the back room, Mona saw her and Sebastian's bodies bound and locked together in the cheval mirror. They looked good together, his tall lean male body curled over her smaller female form. His mouth at her neck. One hand between her legs to caress her clitoris as he slid in and out of her with wet strokes. In the mirror she saw herself on her elbows on the bed, her back arched and Sebastian's hips pumping into her. She wanted to come but she wanted to watch Sebastian come even more. Her nipples brushed the silk of the bedcovers and tightened painfully again. They wanted sucking but they could wait for their turn.

Mona could tell Sebastian was close. His head fell back and he groaned, the first audible sound he'd made since entering her. His hands held her by the pelvis and he jerked her back against him. Mona took the deep thrusts stoically as his curved cock pounded painfully inside her. At the last moment he pulled out of her, took his shaft in hand, and pumped his semen onto her back. Mona watched it happening in the mirror, the pearly spurts covering her skin, Sebastian's face contorted into a mask of ecstasy.

He took a few breaths when it was over, then pushed her

onto her back again. He buried his face into her pussy and ate her. She writhed underneath his mouth, his tongue delving deep into the tender hollow he'd just fucked. It was beautiful to her, seeing his head between her thighs. She had to force herself not to watch him working so she could concentrate on coming. He lapped at her clitoris and she moaned in pleasure and approval.

Her climax built quickly. She'd needed this for weeks. Mona gripped the covers, almost tearing them with her long, manicured red fingernails as she pulled on them. Sebastian's tongue was relentless. He didn't let up at all, not once, until she was screaming from her climax. Her vagina fluttered, grasping at emptiness. She needed to be filled again. Sebastian rose up over her and she saw he was erect again. He started to mount her and she stopped him, smiling, and put him on his back. He let her do it without protest—what man wouldn't?—and she took the cock in her hand and pushed it into her sex, which was still gasping from the orgasm. She moaned like the whore Malcolm had made her, sliding down the rod, taking every inch of it. With her palms flat on the bed by his shoulders, she worked herself up and down the length of him. Sebastian took both of her breasts in his hands, squeezing them, pulling her down to his mouth to suckle the red and tender tips.

Her writhing and contortions proved too much for Sebastian. His hips bucked under hers only a few times before his head fell back and he came again. She was too close to stop.

"Forgive me," he said between breaths. "You're too much for me."

"I need more." Her sex ached. It needed pounding.

"What do you need?" he asked.

"Put your fingers in me and fuck me that way," she said, moving over so he could sit up. She stayed on her hands and

TIFFANY REISZ

knees, spread her thighs, made an offering of her dripping cunt to him. He put two fingers into her hole. It wasn't enough and she told him so. He fucked her with three fingers, then four. The hand, she told him. The whole hand. In the mirror she saw him start in surprise but he did as she asked, turning his hand and sliding it fully into her. She could sense he didn't think she could take so much but her body received the hand, enveloped it, and she groaned in relief when it was inside her all the way up the wrist. She spared another glance at Sebastian in the mirror and saw him staring at his arm inside her in fascinated horror. He'd never done this before. Neither had she, but she'd known instinctively she could take it and she had. She reached behind her, grabbed him by the forearm and showed him how to fuck her with his arm.

This was what she needed, total penetration. She rocked her body on Sebastian's hand, fucking herself, impaling herself, bringing herself to orgasm while he watched her using him. Deep throated groans came out of her as she clawed at the sheets, nearly tearing them. The fist was an immovable object inside her so she moved herself all around, squirming and twisting and contorting herself to make it touch every spot that needed touching. Mona was gone again, lost in the blinding waves of obliterating pleasure. The fist in her was too much to take but too much was what she wanted. She needed the extremities of pleasure and pain. Nothing in the middle would do for her anymore. Malcolm had seen to that.

The climax built to a fever pitch. She could no longer hear her own moaning through the sound of the blood pounding in her ears. Sebastian moved his hand inside her in a gentle spiral that opened her up even more. She came with a sharp single cry. Her interior muscles contracted so hard they forced Sebastian's hand out of her. _____

Mona collapsed onto her side and lay there breathing through her nose. Finally, she was spent. But for how long? If Sebastian touched her again she would want him inside her. The aching between her legs was a permanent fixture now. She would have to get used to it.

Sebastian didn't touch her again. He slid slowly off the bed and found his clothes on the floor. He dressed while she watched. He didn't speak.

"I've horrified you," she said.

"It's not that."

"But it is," she said. "You can admit it."

He paused while buttoning his shirt. "I had imagined it differently, that's all."

"Did you think I was innocent?"

"No." He shook his head. "I thought you were...like a girl. I don't know how to say it."

"If I'm not like a girl, what am I like?"

"Like an animal." He didn't say it like a compliment.

She slowly sat up on the bed and spread her legs wide.

"Your semen is on me and inside me," she said, using her fingers to hold her labia open. "See? If I'm an animal, you're a man who fucks animals."

He glared at her. "You're a whore, aren't you? A whore."

"You knew I was."

"No, I didn't. I thought you had a lover and to please you he gave you gifts."

"He doesn't give me Degas sketches because I fuck him. I fuck him because he gives me Degas sketches."

"Show it to me," he said. "I want to pretend that's why I came over here."

She shrugged and stood up.

"It's in my office," she said.

"You won't put on your clothes?"

"The gallery is closed," she said. "Why should I?"

He followed her to the office. She could see him out of the corner of her eyes trying not to look at her nakedness.

She switched on her desk lamp and placed the sketch before him on the desk. Sebastian studied it a long time without touching it. She saw his pupils dilate and she knew the sketch excited him in a way that fucking her hadn't nor ever could. He was the sort of man who wanted a woman to be a girl and if she was too carnal, too sexual, a woman who challenged his primacy, his lust would turn quickly to hate. And to think she'd once judged Malcolm for preferring whores over other women. Now she understood why he did. She'd rather spread her legs for the Minotaur again than this sanctimonious man-child.

"It's a fake," Sebastian said, standing up straight and crossing his arms over his chest, defiant.

"You're certain?"

"I am. Dead certain."

"I see." She picked up the sketch and made as if to tear it into two pieces. Sebastian lunged and snatched it out of her hand.

"I thought so," she said, then laughed at him.

He slapped her.

She stared at him in shock. It had barely hurt, barely stung. He seemed as surprised by the slap as she. Mona laughed again.

He reached for her and pushed her down onto the desk on her back. Mona spread her legs for him as he unzipped his trousers. He leaned over her and entered her. She came almost immediately. Her breasts bounced as he rammed her repeatedly, spearing her with his cock right into her core. This was hate, not lust, but it felt all the same to her. He fucked her to punish her, to shame her for being too much for him. He fucked her to punish her for having desires he could never satisfy, needs he could never meet, a hole he could never fill no matter how many times or how hard or how deeply he penetrated it. He gripped the back of her knees and spread her legs further, holding her splayed open on the desk before him. It seemed the entire office shook with the force of their fucking. A book fell off the shelves and landed on the floor. The desk drawers rattled. Even Sebastian lost control enough to grunt with each stabbing thrust into her. She grasped his shoulders to steady herself she came again. Her pussy clamped down on his shaft, tight as a hand, and his body bent like a bow when he felt it. He cried out and orgasmed with her.

When it passed, she released his shoulders and lay passively on the desk. He remained inside her, his head down as if weeping or praying or hiding his shame.

"Again?" she asked, lifting her hips to taunt him.

"You disgust me." He wrenched himself out of her and straightened his clothes with his back to her. She wasn't hurt by his words, only disappointed in him. He had desire but no passion. They would never suit and she'd been a fool to think they would.

"I wonder if I'll have a bruise on my cheek tomorrow," she said.

She sat up on the desk and crossed her legs to keep the semen from spilling onto the papers underneath her. Probably too late for that.

He turned around. "I shouldn't have struck you. I'm sorry."

"I hope you find a fine sweet young virgin someday to marry," she said. "And I hope she opens her cunt for your brother and your father and your best friend the minute your back is turned."

She thought he would hit her again, but he didn't. He only picked up his coat and threw it over his arm.

"The sketch is real," he said. "You have my word on that."

"Here, you can have it." She held it out to him. His eyes widened.

"You don't mean it," he said.

"I do."

"It's worth thousands. It's Degas."

"He's your favorite, not mine. Take it."

Slowly he raised his hand and took the sketch from her.

"There," she said. "Now we're exactly the same. You fucked me. I paid you. This is how it works."

His eyes were nearly red with fury. She smiled.

"You are a whore," he said.

"Not today. Today I'm buying. So what does that make you?"

He left her then without another word.

He took the sketch with him.

Mona came off the desk. She didn't want to put her clothes on, didn't want to rejoin the real world. She had tried and failed. The world held nothing for her anymore. She wanted only Malcolm, but she had sent him away, ended their arrangement and she had no idea how to contact him again, how to beg him to come back.

Exhausted, spent, and sorrowful, she walked around to the book on the floor that had fallen while Sebastian had fucked her the final time. Without closing the book, she picked it up and studied the page it had opened to when it fell. The image on the page was of a painting called *Der Blutende*. "The Bleeding Man." The date was 1911 and the artist was Viennese painter Max Oppenheimer, a Jewish artist Hitler had labeled a "degenerate," according to the caption. The painting was of a young man with dark hair. He had some sort of gauzy white garment falling down his thighs, partly revealing his flaccid penis. The man's body was curved to the side as if he were in agony. His eyes glowed with pain and he held his hands to the center of his chest where blood was spattered and spurting. Did the blood come from his hands? Or from a wound on his chest? Apparently no one knew for sure. But Mona knew from one glance that the beautiful young man was bleeding from his heart, and he had to use his own hands to hold the heart and the blood inside himself.

She touched the man's face in the painting and loved him. How could she not love such a perfect picture of a broken heart? She wished she could crawl into the painting, hold his naked body to hers, and seal the wound in his chest with her own flesh.

"Malcolm," she whispered. Was he sending her a message with this painting? Had she broken his heart? Was that what he was trying to tell her?

No. Nonsense. She slammed the book shut and pushed it back onto the shelf. The book had fallen off the shelf because a man had fucked her with all his wounded male pride and the earth shook when a man's ego was wounded. That was all.

She went into the gallery bathroom and washed Sebastian's semen out of her and off of her as best she could before returning to the back room. The bed called to her. She pulled back the covers. Sebastian hadn't exhausted her with sex, but he'd worn her out with his tantrum afterwards. She would sleep and when she woke, she would put it all behind her.

Seconds after her head hit the pillow, she fell deeply into unconsciousness and dreamed she woke and saw Malcolm in the bed at her side. She was happy to see him in her dream, even happier that he was naked. She slid her body on top of his and took his cock inside her. He had his hands on his chest and she tried to move them but he wouldn't let her.

"I missed you," she said as she rode him.

He shook his head. "You banished me."

"I didn't mean to," she said. He felt huge inside her and it was a relief to be filled the way she needed. "You scared me."

"I didn't hurt you," he said.

"I thought you had. But you hadn't." She touched his face, his lips, looked into his eyes so dark as the nights they shared together. "Come back to me, Malcolm. I forgive you. Forgive me too."

"I don't know if I can."

"Why not?"

"Because of this." He dropped his hands from his chest to reveal a grotesque hole, black and red and smoking, and blood pumping from a severed artery.

She screamed herself awake.

Mona sat up in the bed. She shook all over. Clenching a pillow to her chest, she rocked back and forth, back and forth, trying to bring herself to her senses.

"Malcolm…" She said his name into the pillow as if she could conjure him with words and wanting.

Was she losing her mind? She almost thought she was. It was the only thing that made sense. Was Malcolm even real? Had she dreamed all of it? No. There were the paintings as proof. The paintings and the etchings and the sketches proved he'd been here. She had to see him again. She would die if she didn't.

She left the bed and walked into her office, switched on the Tiffany lamp once more. In her coat closet she found a wrap sweater and pulled it on to keep her warm while she worked. She took the wine bottle she'd tossed into the wastepaper basket, uncorked it and dumped the fragments of the white card onto the desk. In her desk drawer she found tape. For the next hour she set about putting the pieces of the white card back together. The ragged tears and porous paper made the task maddeningly difficult but she didn't stop, not even when Tou-Tou jumped on the desk and scattered some of the pieces. She didn't know why she did it, only that she had to get a message to Malcolm. How he saw her, she didn't know. How he watched her, how he seemingly knew she'd gone out with Sebastian to the exhibit...all mysteries. But he watched her, that much she knew. He saw what she did and who she did it with...and he'd see her message.

She had to have him back.

Finally, it was finished. Every piece back in place, taped down so that it looked like a Frankenstein card. She found her clothes and put them on, picked up Tou-Tou and put him in the large leather handbag that doubled as his carrier. She left the card on the bed and went home to her apartment.

There was nothing left to do but wait for him.

That night she dreamt of *The Bleeding Man* again. In the second dream he died while inside of her and the red was everywhere, on her hands and on her chest and on her mouth as she drank the blood straight from his heart.

IX: ROMAN CHARITY

On the Ides of March, Malcolm finally made contact with her again.

She'd just closed the gallery for the evening, which entailed nothing more than drawing the red velvet curtains behind the front windows, flipping the OPEN sign around, and locking the door. Upon returning to her office to fetch Tou-Tou from his basket, she found a book of art lying open on her desk. It had been so long since she'd seen Malcolm, she'd almost given up hope he'd ever return to her. She glanced around the office, sniffing the air, hoping to catch any glimpse of him, any trace of his scent. Her body came alive merely at the possibility of Malcolm. As ecstatic as she was that he wanted to see her again, she feared to open the book. What did he want with her this time? What would he make her do? What would he do to her? What would he make her enjoy him doing to her?

She sat in her desk chair slowly and told herself she was doing it for the money. For the money she would see Malcolm again. For the money she would submit to his sexual demands. For the money she would open the book.

But it wasn't for the money.

She opened the book anyway.

The red velvet cord marked a page near the back. On it was a painting called *Roman Charity*, dated 1767 by the artist Jean-Baptiste Greuze. She'd never seen the painting before or heard the phrase "Roman charity." It meant nothing to her, but the scene was clear enough. A thin old man languished in a prison cell and a young woman in a voluminous dress offered him her breast to suckle. A prostitute visiting a prisoner? Seemed like a logical explanation for the scene. It was tame enough. Bare breasts hardly shocked her. After the Minotaur nothing could shock her.

In her head she heard Malcolm's voice taunting her.

Don't say things like that. Men like me take statements such as that as a challenge.

Mona still didn't know what had happened the night with the Minotaur. Had he drugged her with an untraceable drug? Or had the wine been potent enough to daze her into seeing the back room as the meeting place for ancient Athenian priestesses and the Minotaur they served? Or was there another possibility far more terrifying than being drugged or going mad?

What if—somehow, some way, some impossible way—it had all been real?

Mona knew that question would plague her the rest of her life if she never learned the answer, and she would never learn the answer if she never saw Malcolm again. Reason told her to run, to escape this dangerous game she was playing with this dangerous man. But she was past reason now. She'd had the strongest orgasm of her life while chained to a boulder with a half-man, half-beast inside her. There was no going back after that. She could only go forward.

After gathering Tou-Tou in his carrier, she went to her

apartment. She had some of her mother's old gala dresses hanging in the closet. One was blood purple with bell sleeves and full skirts with gold braiding on the bodice. It looked like something from a late Renaissance painting. As soon as she put it on and stepped in front of the mirror, Mona felt an overwhelming compulsion to return to the gallery that very night. She tried to ignore the compulsion, but it grew stronger when she unbuttoned the back of her dress. It felt like an itch, only inside her brain where she could never reach it. Quickly she buttoned the dress again and the itch lessened. She took a step toward the door and it lessened more. She walked away from the door and sat on her bed and the itch grew so strong she wanted to beat her head into her hands. There was nothing for it. She had to go.

The streets were almost empty at this late hour, yet she still received her fair share of strange glances in her dress with the skirts so flowing she had to hold them up to avoid tripping over the hem as she half-walked, half-ran back to The Red.

She entered by the side door and didn't hesitate a second before slipping through the door into the back room.

But the back room she knew was gone.

"Malcolm...what have you done?" she whispered as she the door closed behind her.

For surely Malcolm had done this deed. But how? The wood flooring was gone, replaced by hard stone. The walls were stone as well. Flaming torches lined the stone walls and the smell of burning wood pricked at her nostrils. She could see the dark night sky through a square, iron-barred window chiseled in the stone. She pressed her back to the wall when she saw two men approaching. They were carrying bronze helmets under their arms, and wore dull white tunics and leather sandals. They looked like how she'd always pictured ancient Roman soldiers.

"You there," one said to her. "Coming or going?"

She panicked. "Coming," she said. "But I don't—"

"Cimon's girl," the other said. "Let her pass. He's not long for the world."

"I'll search her. You know our orders."

She shrank from his hands when they reached for her but she knew she must not fight as her body was bent over and searched. Searched for what? For weapons? Her? She had nothing. The soldier ran his hands all over her body and through her clothes. The two soldiers smiled at each other as the one lingered longer than necessary under her skirts where she was bare and naked. Mona warmed to his touch. Malcolm had trained her to enjoy being violated and this man was certainly violating her. He cupped her bottom, rubbed it, slid his hand between her thighs and pushed one finger into her.

"I don't have anything," she said as he stuck in a second finger and stroked her inner walls. "I swear I don't."

"Let her pass," the older soldier said. "We have to finish our rounds."

"If we must," the younger one said, taking his hand out from under her skirt. He pointed at an open doorway with the fingers that had just been inside her. "Hurry. He's not going to last much longer."

"Thank you," she said, dipping into a curtsy. She rushed past the men and down the passageway. Torches lit her way, although she didn't know where her way led. Cimon? Who was Cimon? The man in the painting? The prisoner? She was there for Malcolm, but who knew what role he'd decided to play in this carnal Wonderland.

She heard low moans coming from the rooms she passed. They weren't moans of pleasure but of profoundest suffering. This was a prison. She understood that. And somewhere in this prison was Malcolm, waiting for her. The panic in her heart was real. Her lungs pounded with it. Her dress felt tight across her chest. Her breasts ached horribly, and she wondered if it was because her panicked breathing was constricting her blood flow. They felt congested, swollen. Ignoring her pain, she ran down the dust-choked corridor until she came to the very end.

The cell was not guarded and the iron door wasn't locked. She looked around to see if anyone would stop her from entering. She saw no one. She took a torch from a wall sconce and entered through the open door.

"Malcolm?" she whispered. The room was dark and dank and cold. She heard the rattling of a chain on the stone floor and she inched toward the sound. "Malcolm? Oh, God, Malcolm..."

It was him, though he hardly looked himself. He lay naked but for a loincloth on the cold floor, his knees pulled to his chest and his hair the white of dirty snow. His body was skeletal. She could see every bone and every sinew and every joint. The withered face was unmistakably her Malcolm, his black eyes glinting like flint. He had not lost his will to live, though it seemed he had lost everything else. His only possession was the iron shackle on his ankle that bound him by a thick chain of heavy links to the wall. Mona put the torch into the wall sconce and knelt on the floor by his head. She touched his face tenderly and wept.

"What's happening?" she asked. "What have they done to you?"

He opened his lips but no sound came out. She looked for water, for wine, for anything to wet his tongue. The dungeon was empty but for his broken body.

"Starved," he whispered.

"Oh, God." Mona gathered his shivering body to hers. She could have counted his ribs with her fingers in the dark he was so thin. She wrapped him as best she could in her thick skirts.

"Food," he said, and it sounded like he was trying to ask her a question.

"I have nothing," she said. "They searched me."

He nodded, resigned to his death, and closed his eyes.

She rocked him against her like a baby in her arms. He was so frail, so helpless, it made her heart ache. The pain in her breasts grew unbearable. She wept in sorrow and in pain. Malcolm rested his head on her chest and she groaned under a fresh wave of agony. Something was happening. She felt the front of her dress grow damp and warm. Was Malcolm bleeding on her? Frantically, she pushed the bodice of the dress down. She saw no blood, only her breasts, red and swollen and her nipples distended. The fluid was leaking from her breasts. White fluid, not red.

At once she understood the painting and the meaning of *Roman Charity*. It wasn't a painting of a prostitute paying a conjugal visit to a prisoner. It was a painting of a woman feeding a starving prisoner from her own breasts. Without a second thought she took her breast in her hand and lifted it to his mouth.

"Suck," she told him, but he seemed too weak to hear her. She tilted his head gently forward and cradled him in her arms like a child. The guards had searched her body for food but they couldn't take the food from inside her body. Malcolm slowly parted his lips. She pressed her nipple into his mouth, and this time he was able to latch onto her breast. She wrapped her skirts around him even more, hiding this private act from prying eyes lest they rip her away from him and the nourishment that would keep him alive. As he nursed from her breast, her pain eased. She kissed his forehead, his hollowed cheeks as he drank from her body. As the minutes passed, he seemed to gain strength. His thin hand clutched her bare shoulder as he drank more deeply of her. By the firelight of the torch, his hair darkened from white to gray and slowly, ever so slowly, to black again.

When he'd emptied one breast, she shifted him in her arms, pressing her other breast into his mouth. He latched on far more quickly this time and she wept with relief. He would live. She had saved him.

"What crime did you commit?" she whispered. "Why are you here?"

"I loved a woman I shouldn't have loved," he said, so quietly she wouldn't have heard him but for the echo of his words off the stone walls.

"And you were imprisoned because of that? Starved?"

He nodded and took her nipple into his mouth again and suckled.

"Did I hurt you?" she asked.

"Yes," he said against her breast. "Not your fault."

Her hot tears fell on his face as he nursed. She asked him no more questions as he fed from her. She'd never known such terrible tenderness as she knew now with his frail body in her arms and her body feeding his in this most intimate of ways. Holding him in her arms, nursing him from her breasts, she knew she did love him, though what that meant for them she didn't know. Nothing made sense. All of this was impossible. How could she lactate like this without ever having had a child?

At last he seemed sated. He released his hold on her breast and lay his head back in her arms. She rocked him like a mother with a child, though the words she whispered were the words of lovers.

"Forgive me," she said to him. Though his body was still thin and weak, his face was again the face of the man she'd seen in the gallery the first night, the face of a man at the prime of his life.

"It isn't your fault," he said. "You didn't know what you were doing to me when you brought him to our bed."

"Sebastian." She sighed. "I was angry at you. I wanted to be with someone else so I could pretend I didn't want you anymore. I didn't think I could hurt you."

"I felt it happening," he said. He sounded like a man recovering from a long illness. His voice wavered, weak and tired, but he would live. "It was like…bleeding. Bleeding out."

"How? How did you feel it?"

He shook his head. "I can't explain. Not yet."

"I want to have your child," she said. "Will you do that for me? You said you would leave me, but I want to have your child whether you stay or go. Can I?"

"You may have my child. It's what I've wanted all along, for you to have the next heir."

"Why?"

"A deathbed promise."

"What was the promise?"

"I can't explain."

"Not yet?"

"Not yet," he said. "But you'll understand soon enough."

"I can wait," she said. "I trust you now."

"That's all I ask."

"Do you need more?" she asked. As soon as he told her he would let her have his child, her breasts felt painfully full again. He nodded and she lowered her bodice again, giving him her breast. The milk flowed into his mouth. By some magic his rail-thin body filled out until he was once again whole and healthy and he looked himself again, proud and virile. She didn't question it or fear this magic anymore. It simply was.

"I'll have a son." As soon as she said it she knew she wasn't dreaming of the future but seeing it. Somewhere a house made of stone awaited her, iron gates, and a garden of red-thorned roses. "He'll take after you. I'll name him anything you tell me to name him."

"Name him for me," he said before returning to her breast.

She nodded, smiled. Her son would be named Malcolm, after his father. And she would nurse the son like she'd nursed the father and she would love them both until the day she died.

Mona wrapped her arms around Malcolm to hide them from view. She'd heard footsteps in the corridor and feared discovery.

"I must help you," she said.

"Let me inside you," he said.

That was easily enough done. She pushed him gently onto his back and straddled his stomach as he lifted her skirts to her waist. With one finger he stroked her, splitting her along the seam of her sex with his fingers. The folds parted for him easily as he touched her. As soon as she'd grown wet enough, he positioned his cock at her opening and eased her down onto it.

Mona wept with joy to have him inside her again. Her purple skirts made a blanket for them and under that blanket they coupled themselves together, deeply, slowly, and with such tenderness she feared she'd never stop crying. Malcolm kissed her face, her tears, her hair that spilled over her shoulders. Somehow—he didn't tell her and she knew he wouldn't —somehow she knew he'd been languishing, a prisoner, all this time. She'd fed him through their lovemaking and when she'd taken it away from him, she'd starved him somehow. Someone else had made him a prisoner but it was she who'd taken his sustenance from him.

"I'll never banish you again," she said as she moved up and down on him. She clenched her inner muscles, wanting to hold him tight inside of her and never let him out. "You scared me so much that night. Was that your true form?"

"Only the form of my soul," he said. "A prisoner, deformed, half animal."

"You're beautiful to me," she said. "I'll do whatever it takes to free you."

"The time will come when I'll ask you to do something you don't want to do again."

"I don't care. I'll do it anyway. There's nothing you could ask me to do that I won't allow."

"Will you let me go when it's time?"

"If you'll leave me your child in your place, then yes," she said. "But please don't ask that of me, my love."

"You don't love me."

"I do, I swear I do." She showered his face with kisses. "Tell me how to prove it and I'll prove it to you."

"When I must leave you, you'll know what to do."

"Then when you leave me, I'll do it."

Though he was whole and healthy again, he still nursed from her breasts. She knew once they were empty they wouldn't be full again until she'd had his child. She didn't know what magic made this possible but she didn't question it. She'd never felt closer to a lover, not even those long nights with Ryan inside her, shielding her from the reality of her mother's illness. Malcolm pushed her gown down to her waist and ran his hands along her bare back. The floor was hard and cold underneath them and tore at her knees, but to her it was finer than any luxurious bed since Malcolm was inside her again.

Beneath her, Malcolm lifted his hips, pushing into her from below. She held perfectly still as he rocked his hips and pounded into her. It was heaven to take him, to spread her thighs and open herself to receive all of him. He reached under her dress again, found her clitoris and kneaded it. The pleasure was unbearable. She could hardly stay silent as he took her, fully in control of her body even as he lay on his back chained to the wall. His money had made her a whore, but his cock had made her his slave. She never wanted to taste freedom again. She only wanted to taste him.

"Come for me," he said into her ear. He took her breast in his mouth again and sucked it while he stroked her under her skirts. A low soft moan emanated from the back of her throat and the contractions began. Her wet inner walls clenched and released before they were seized with a violent fluttering that dragged on and on. She felt it in her back, in her thighs, in the inmost parts of her. At last it passed and she collapsed onto him, her sore breasts pressed into his chest.

She kissed his mouth, his lovely mouth, and the kiss was lovely and loving. He took her by the waist and lifted her off of him.

"Now me," he said. "Drink from me."

It was her pleasure to do it. She slid down his body and took him into her mouth, tasting herself on his shaft. She wasted no time on the usual niceties but pulled the organ down her throat and sucked hard. He arched on the floor, his hips lifting, and he exploded into her mouth. As he came she pulled the semen out of him, sucking it down her throat, every drop, emptying his body as he'd emptied hers. After it was done she lay her head on his stomach and held his cock in her hand, cradling it between her naked breasts.

"How do I free you from this place?" she whispered. The guards would find them together like this any minute. She knew they would expel her and torture him for what they'd done together.

"Open your eyes," he said.

She did as ordered and lifted her head. They were in the bed in the back room again. The iron chain on his ankle was gone. He looked like himself again, like her Malcolm, her lover, her owner, her god.

She glanced around the room, blinking, stupefied.

"How do you do it all?" she asked. "How do you make me see what I see?"

"You see what I see," he said.

"Is it real?"

"It's real enough."

"Are you the devil?" she asked, knowing that the answer—yes or no—would change nothing between them.

"Do you believe in the devil?" Malcolm asked.

"No, but Mother did. Heaven and hell and anything fantastical, she believed in it all. Beauty over truth, always."

"Not all that is beautiful is untrue, Mona."

Malcolm took her by the waist and pulled her to him. He laid her on her back, lifted her skirts to her stomach and put his hand into her wet sex. It sank into her to his wrist. Her body stretched to accommodate him and once it had, it closed around his hand again, enveloping him, holding him within her where he belonged. She'd made Sebastian perform this very act on her and he had done so reluctantly and been horrified by it. Not Malcolm. He looked at her with near reverence as he worked his hand carefully in deeper.

"Why did you come to me?" she asked, resting her hand on the side of his face. "Why were you waiting for me? Why me? I'm not special. I'm not…anything."

"Long ago I made a deathbed promise. I need you to help me keep it as I'm helping you to keep yours. I promise, you will understand in time, Mona. You'll understand it all."

She saw the truth in his eyes. Someday she would know who he was and when she knew who he was she would finally know herself. Tonight, it didn't matter. She knew she was his and that was enough. Mona closed her eyes and rested her head back against the pillow. Malcolm filled her so entirely there was no space left inside her for doubts or fears. He kissed the tops of her still swollen breasts, and she smiled languidly. He had drained her and the emptiness was simply another aching void for him to fill.

"You're tired, love," he said. "Go to sleep. It's almost dawn."

"If I fall asleep, you'll leave me again."

"I've never left you when you slept."

"But when I wake you're not here."

"When you wake you can't see me. But I'm here. I'm always here."

"Make me come again and I'll sleep."

"You're terribly greedy."

"For you," she said. "Only greedy for you."

He kissed her lips lightly and moved his head between her legs. With his hand inside her, he only lapped lightly at her clitoris to bring her to climax. Her sex quivered around his hand, squeezing it, holding it. It was ecstasy beyond words to be filled up so completely. She never wanted to be empty again and she told him that. When his hand slipped out of her at last, he replaced it with his cock. He rode her with long, slow strokes, seemingly endless. If only they were.

"I dreamed you were dead," she said, half-asleep and falling fast as he rocked her with his deep and gentle thrusts. "I'm afraid I'll dream that again."

"You won't dream that tonight, I promise."

"Is this all a dream? That's the only thing that makes any sense."

"You aren't dreaming," he said, and she knew that was true. She was awake and had been every time they had met.

"But if it were a dream, would you want to wake up?" he asked.

A good question. A fair question. A hard question, but one she answered easily.

"Never."

X: THE LUNCHEON ON THE GRASS

*I*t wasn't a dream. Mona knew that for certain. Nor was she insane. Nor had Malcolm drugged her. She didn't know the source of Malcolm's magic and she could not begin to guess the purpose of his tricks or the prestige, but she knew what she'd seen and felt was real, as real as anything had ever been in her life and likely ever would be.

She woke alone in the bed at the gallery. Her insides were sore from Malcolm's hand, but her breasts felt normal. Her sleep had been dreamless. There was a lightness to her step once again, as the dark cloud over her had lifted.

The happiness didn't fade even as the long days and lonely nights passed. She was certain she would see Malcolm again and sure enough, the day came when she found a book of paintings on her desk and Malcolm waiting for her in the back room. A few weeks passed and he came to her again. Their nights together were passionate and fulfilling but no longer terrifying. He conjured no monsters, dragged her into no hells. She sensed he'd been testing her in some way and finally she had passed. Malcolm came to her in April and twice in May. The first of June arrived and she woke up fearful. The first time he'd come to her had been in late June of last year. It was almost over, whatever this game was.

He'd made her three promises when they'd made their deal: He promised to pay her enough in art to save the gallery. He promised to tell her the provenance of the paintings.

And he promised he would leave her.

She refused to think of the final promise. Surely the terms of the agreement had changed. She'd told him she loved him, told him she wanted to have his baby, and he'd told her that he would allow that someday. She held onto those words, treasuring them like a talisman. And she needed that talisman once the banks started calling again. She had nearly a dozen valuable and important sketches and etchings she could sell once she had provenance, she assured them. All she needed now was Malcolm's name and the story he hadn't yet told her.

By the middle of June, the city was sweating again. Even when it rained, the sidewalks steamed in the heat. Mona rarely left the shady coolness of her gallery for her apartment. She'd never lain with Malcolm there, so it felt like a foreign country to her, whereas The Red was her home.

On a Sunday morning she woke up to a city burning in the heat and she fled straight to the gallery hours before it opened. In her office she found a book lying on her desk, marked with the red velvet ribbon. Mona laughed, her heart bubbling, when she saw the painting he had marked in the book. Manet again. How fitting to return to Manet one year after their first night together. The painting was famous, more famous even than *Olympia*. Known as *Le Déjeuner sur l'herbe*—"The Luncheon on the Grass"—it was the painting her mother jokingly called "The *Other* Naked Lunch."

Two men, fully dressed, reclined on the grass, having

what seemed to be an intense conversation. Sitting next to the men and staring directly at the viewer was a woman, entirely naked. The men paid no attention to her nor to the woman behind them bathing in a stream. Mona wondered if the painting was Manet's commentary on the art establishment, more interested in talk than the world around them. The woman was nature in the raw and the men wanted nothing to do with her. It didn't surprise her in the least that Malcolm would want to recreate such a painting and rectify what he undoubtedly considered a moral failing on the part of the men.

Curious, Mona walked to the back room door and peeked inside. Malcolm had wasted no time preparing for the assignation. Instead of wooden floors, she found lush green grass under her feet. Instead of a ceiling, she saw a hazy blue sky. And instead of walls, she saw a silver stream through the trees. The day was halcyon. It looked like someone's memory of a perfect day. She gazed around her and saw that nothing remained of the back room but the door, freestanding, like a portal to another world. Now she understood that in some mysterious way it was. Another world of Malcolm's creation.

Somewhere close by people talked. She heard their voices, low but unmistakably male. Mona undressed, dropping her silk skirt and blouse onto the grass. She walked barefoot and naked toward the sound of the men. She spied them before they spied her, sitting beside their picnic blanket in their black suits as they exchanged friendly fire over something silly and political. Malcolm she recognized at once. The other man seemed familiar, but she knew her mind was tricking her. She'd never seen him before. She hid herself behind the tree and studied him. He had dark reddish-brown hair in a modern Brutus cut. His eyes were dark, but not black like Malcolm's. They were midnight blue instead—she was sure of it even from a distance. Midnight blue eyes and a midnight smile as he spoke. He seemed the sort of man who made all his business deals in a bedroom, not a boardroom. He had a strong nose, strong chin, and strong jaw beneath his beard, and looked a little younger than Malcolm—thirty-five, maybe. Everything about him exuded quiet strength. He was desperately handsome, and in that alone he reminded her of Malcolm. He wore a ring on his left ring finger, but it wasn't a wedding ring. It looked like an antique signet ring of sorts, large, ornately engraved, and silver.

Mona stepped into the clearing where the two men sat chatting. Malcolm glanced her way and waved her over, patting the blanket at his side. She sat, slightly self-conscious of her nakedness even as she knew the other man with the signet ring was nothing more than a figment of Malcolm's imagination. He wasn't real any more than the little pastel nymphs or the men who'd bid on her at the slave auction. He was no more real than the Roman prison guard who'd searched her body, no more real than the priestesses who served the Minotaur.

Malcolm placed his hand on her thigh as she stretched out on the blanket.

"It's got to go," Malcolm was saying to the other man. "It's outdated, outmoded. It's a relic."

"Of course it's a relic," the man with the midnight eyes said. "I'm not arguing that point."

"What is your point?" Malcolm asked.

"My point is…people love their relics. Don't they?" the midnight man asked, turning to Mona.

"You're asking me?" she said.

"You run an art gallery, don't you?" he asked.

"She does," Malcolm said.

"Then you know better than either of us that people love relics," the midnight man said. "What painting would sell for more money—a bad painting that's four hundred years old, or a good painting that was finished yesterday?"

"The four-hundred-year old painting," she said. "Almost always."

"See?" the midnight man said. "My point is proven. The monarchy remains intact."

"You're trying to end the monarchy?" she asked Malcolm. "A strange quest for an Englishman."

"He's a strange Englishman," the midnight man said.

"It's a relic of a benighted age," Malcolm said.

"So is everything valuable that you detest," the midnight man said. "Including marriage."

"I surrender," Malcolm said.

Mona laughed at them. They seemed to be dear old friends, though Malcolm had yet to introduce her to his friend.

"Let's talk of something more pleasant than my two least favorite M words," Malcolm said. "Let us talk of my favorite M word."

"Which is?" Mona asked.

Malcolm leaned over and kissed her softly on the lips.

"Mona," he said.

"A much better topic of conversation indeed," the midnight man said. Mona looked at him and found him at her other side. She stiffened when he leaned in to kiss her as well. She assumed he was there to be an audience to her and Malcolm's lovemaking. It seemed he was to participate as well. Malcolm had never let anyone else have sex with her in these fantasies he conjured for her. Would that change today?

"Trust me, love," Malcolm said, and it was all she needed to hear. The man with the midnight eyes smiled at her and Mona found herself returning the smile, her naked body blushing crimson. It was all a fantasy anyway, wasn't it? He was a figment of Malcolm's imagination, a figment who would be gone the moment she returned to the outside world.

The midnight man kissed her mouth, a kiss both tender and cruel. He held her chin in his hand so that she couldn't move away from his lips (not that she wanted to). His tongue probed the inside of her mouth as if she were something the man had purchased sight unseen and wanted to see if he'd gotten his money's worth. She grew warm as he kissed her, warm and then hot. He pushed her gently but forcefully onto her back and kept kissing her. As he kissed her, Malcolm fondled her. She would know his touch blindfolded in the dark. He fondled her breasts while she and the midnight man kissed deeply, his beard tickling her chin and cheeks. Malcolm rolled her nipples around his fingers until they hardened painfully, and when they were too sensitive she thought she would scream, he took one in his mouth and suckled it. She moaned into the midnight man's mouth and he chuckled at her ardor.

"Beautiful whore," the midnight man said. "I may have to keep you."

He laughed again softly before kissing her again roughly. If it were possible, and she doubted it was, the man seemed even more arrogant than Malcolm. She was starting to like him. His tongue touched hers and she felt something electric pass between them. It made her heart jump and her stomach tremble. Or perhaps that was merely from Malcolm's touch on her naked body as he trailed a hand from her breasts to her thighs and up again.

Malcolm pressed her legs apart and lay between her thighs. She tried to break the kiss when Malcolm opened her labia and licked her, but the midnight man didn't allow it. He forced her to keep kissing him even as Malcolm lapped at her clitoris. The kiss turned into the sweetest form of torture as Malcolm played with her vagina, rubbing along the front wall and pushing his fingertips gently into her most shivering and sensitive places. To kiss and come at the same time was nearly impossible, but the two men seemed intent on forcing her to do it.

The man with the midnight eyes took her breast in his hand and squeezed it while he deepened the kiss even further, delving into her mouth with his tongue as if to eat her every moan. He tasted like he'd been drinking honeyed wine and eating freshly plucked pears—an intoxicating, delicious mix, like sangria. She opened her mouth wider to him as Malcolm pried her tight pussy open with his thumb and forefinger. She moaned into her new lover's mouth and she felt him trying not to smile.

Mona sensed Malcolm moving. She couldn't see what he was doing as the kiss prevented her from raising her head. But she felt it, felt him put the thick tip of his cock into her. She tried lifting her hips, eager for more of him, but he held her down on the ground. He brought his mouth onto her left breast again and sucked. The midnight man kissed her along her jawline, nibbled her earlobe and finally took her right breast into his mouth. Never in her life had two different men sucked her at the same time. Her head fell back and she arched on the ground. Yes…this was it, bliss beyond words. These two hot sucking mouths and her body their property and possession. The man with the midnight eyes took her breast in his hand and squeezed it. He plucked at the nipple. He tugged it and twisted it, not viciously but not gently, and the sensation pieced her chest all the way to her back. The man with the midnight eyes stared at her breast while he fondled and sucked her. He seemed to find her mesmerizing, almost as if he were as surprised to be here doing this deed as she was. Who was he? He seemed far more substantial than the shades and shadows of people Malcolm had conjured in his other fantasies. He breathed the word "lovely" before kissing her nipple again. She twined her fingers into his rust-colored hair. She found him impossibly beautiful. Malcolm had done well with this fantasy man. Perhaps Malcolm had read her mind and found her ideal lover. She wouldn't put it past him.

She turned her head and saw Malcolm looking at her, her nipple deep in his mouth. She touched his face with her fingertips and smiled lovingly at him. He raised his head, smiled back at her, and then thrust his cock into her so hard she saw crimson stars in front of her eyes.

"Devil..." she said, and Malcolm chuckled fiendishly.

The man with the midnight eyes put his mouth at her ear. "He's terrible, isn't he?" he whispered. "But do you want to know something?"

"Tell me," she said.

"I'm worse."

She saw in his eyes he meant it, but where was the fun in taking him at his word?

"Prove it," she said.

Those dark blue eyes of his widened in surprise and his pupils dilated with desire. "I must be dreaming," he said.

"Why is that?" she asked.

"Because you're my dream girl."

He lowered his head to her mouth again before she could say another word. He groped her breast while kissing her, while Malcolm fucked her wet cunt. The organ inside her was rapture. Malcolm had her legs up on his shoulders to send the broad and firm tip sliding into the deepest parts of her.

"You should be like this all the time," the midnight man said against her lips. "Naked with a cock stuck in you. You wear it well."

"Do I?" she asked, hardly knowing what she said as she was so lost in the moment.

"Your breasts are rose red and your nipples are wine. I can't wait to find out what shade of red your cunt is."

"It'll be red and white when I'm done with her," Malcolm said. "A candy cane."

"Or the flag of Sweden," Mona said. "Or is it Denmark?"

"I'll leave you blue bruises and it'll be the flag of America, England, and France," Malcolm said. "And I will salute them all."

"No." The midnight man shook his head, caressed her lips. "A Wingthorn rose. White flowers, but the thorns are blood red and large as the petals. Beautiful and dangerous as I imagine getting in your cunt is."

"You'll be ensnared too," Malcolm said. "But you won't want to ever get out again."

Mona laughed, drunk on happiness, drunk on lust.

"Come and get in here, lad," Malcolm said. "You'll see what I mean."

Malcolm pulled out of her and lowered her legs to the blanket again. He stretched out on his side next to her. The man with midnight eyes took Malcolm's place between her legs. It pleased her to spread her thighs and display herself to him. With both hands he fanned her labia open, splaying her wide for his perusal and inspection.

"Apple red," he said, nodding his approval. "The color that tempted both Adam and Eve. Do you taste as sweet as you look?" he asked, but didn't wait for her answer. He dipped his head and licked her inner lips, swirling his tongue in circles all over her. He poked his tongue into the open orifice once before raising up again. "Even sweeter than I thought. Sweet and tart. Consider me a fallen man."

He pulled off his jacket and tossed it aside. Then he opened his trousers and brought out his prick, already fully erect. Mona's breathing quickened at the sight of it, dark red and straining in his hand. A beautiful male organ, it was long and thick as his wrist, and her craving for it grew as he stroked it.

"Open yourself for me," the man with the midnight eyes ordered. She spread her labia for him as he had, using her hands to expose the hole. He mounted her, placing the cock at her entrance and holding it in place with his hand. With one purposeful thrust, he penetrated her to her core and proceeded to fuck her without further preamble. He grasped her by the thigh and wrapped her leg around his back, then dug into her with vigorous strokes. He was over her and under her at the same time, having tilted her pelvis up so far he could slip his knees under her hips to better impale her. Mona tried to touch him but he grabbed her by the wrists and imprisoned her against the blanket. He gave no quarter, this man with midnight blue eyes, brooked no dissent. There was no question of respite or mercy. She existed solely to take his cock and like it, and the second part was optional.

Mona released short sharp breaths as the man rammed her with his iron cock. Her inner muscles tightened and twisted, grasping at the shaft, lavishing it with wetness and attention and adoration. She could barely stand the building pressure. Malcolm added to her torment by lightly pulling back on the hood of her clitoris, exposing the swollen knot of tissue beneath. It pulsed against Malcolm's fingers, pulsed in time to the powerful thrusts that split her down the seams with each thrust. Inhuman sounds emanated from her lips. Her belly tightened. Her thighs tightened. Seeing Malcolm's fingers on her clitoris, the midnight man's organ disappearing into her, and her heavy swollen breasts rising and falling with each rough thrust was too much for Mona. She saw too much, felt too much, was taking far too much to survive it. And just when she couldn't take anymore, they gave her more.

They gave her more.

The man with the midnight eyes lifted her in his arms, clasping her to his chest even as his penis remained inside her. She wrapped her arms around him, holding him as tightly as he held her. He rolled onto his back, and as soon as she found herself on top of him, Mona began to ride him. She put her hands on his chest and arched her back, displaying her breasts for him, offering them to him for sucking and touching. She screwed her hips in a circle, grinding on the organ inside her. Without warning, the man underneath her bucked his hips and lifted her. He caught her before she collapsed onto his chest, caught her and held her against him again. She fought the arms that held her. She needed to move, to reach her climax. It was killing her not to come. The man was ten times stronger than she, however, and kept her trapped against his chest. He slid his hands up and down her back as she panted like an animal in heat. He took her bottom in his hands and spread her at the cleft. Mona gasped when she felt something cool and wet against her anus, but she knew the fingers that touched her. Malcolm's fingers penetrated her second hole slowly. She sighed at this loveliest of violations. He oiled her again, oiled her thoroughly. First he used only one finger, but when her anus opened up to him he pushed in a second. Soon she was able to take three of his fingers. He worked those three fingers into her until she took them with ease. He fucked her with them as the man underneath started to move again inside her. In tandem they fucked her, sliding in together and out in unison. When they both left her holes she could have wept from the aching emptiness, but in a flash they were entering her again and she sighed with happiness, unbearable happiness.

The man underneath her locked his legs together and Malcolm rose up, covering her back to take her from behind. The fingers were gone soon and quickly replaced with

Malcolm's cock. She knew this act was inevitable and while she wanted it, she also feared it. Malcolm read her tension and soothed her with a series of kisses across her naked shoulders.

"Open up for me," he whispered and she spread her thighs as wide as she could. Movement became impossible and unnecessary when both men were fully within her. She was pinned into place by their pricks. Mona buried her head into the crook of the midnight man's strong neck and lay there taking it all in as the two men used her holes in tandem.

It was an obscenity, this act, being fucked by two men at once in both her holes. She felt the two organs separated only by a wall of sensitive tissue that quivered between them, spasmed and flinched. Staked by these twin spears she could do nothing but remain motionless and receive. She dug her fingers into the fine linen fabric of the midnight man's shirt and clung to him as if for life. His breathing was ragged, desperate, hungry and music to her ears. Soft moans lived and died in his throat. She'd never heard sounds so erotic. She looked at him and saw his eyes were closed and his lips were parted and she couldn't stop herself from kissing that mouth that still tasted of everything red and tempting.

"If you were for sale I would pawn my soul to buy you," the midnight man said into her ear. "I would buy you and keep you a naked slave chained to my bed. I would show off your cunt to every man who crossed the threshold of my house so they could see my prized possession and envy me. I would fuck beautiful women in front of you and send them home right after, still dripping with my seed, so you would know that I could have any girl I wanted but you were the only one I wanted to keep. I would tie you to the dining room table and drink my wine out of you. I would let my dearest friends bend you over the billiard table and fuck your pussy and arse while I sat in my favorite club chair, sipping

Scotch and watching you writhe for my entertainment. Then later when I'm fucking you in our bed, you can tell me in exquisite detail how much you prefer my cock to theirs. And if you're a very good little girl, I would share you like this, a cock in both holes—and if and when you're an angel to me, I'll let you take a cock in all three. You're a magnificent whore and I'd love to wrap you around my cock every day for the rest of your life."

The words were too much for Mona. Her vagina contracted so hard she cried out. Her stomach muscles rippled. Electric currents shot up her spine to the back of her neck. Her thighs quivered and she shook without moving. The climax with two organs deep in her was devastating. She'd never recover from it. It went on forever and when it stopped she thought she'd died for a moment.

"I knew you two would get along," Malcolm said as he continued to mercilessly plumb the depths of her.

Mona rested her head on the midnight man's chest and felt the low rumble of his laughter. The two men continued to use her without her active participation. Her holes were wet and open. What more did they require from her but acquiescence? Malcolm's hands scored her naked back and she shivered like a cat being scratched just the right way. The midnight man pumped into her, lifting her by his cock with each thrust. They were building toward the crisis, holding back, then pushing forward together. Her whole being was concentrated now in her pelvis, in the two holes they were using and nothing else. She lay limp on the midnight man's body and waited for them to finish with her. The sooner they finished, the sooner it would all begin again.

Malcolm's hand gripped the back of her neck, not hard but possessively. His thrusts slowed and deepened. He was almost there. She could tell it from the sounds he made—the guttural moans had turned to long low breaths. The grip on her neck tightened. Malcolm came into her, his hot spurts filling her bowels, while underneath her the midnight man lifted his hips off the ground and released into her at the same time. She froze, held her breath, felt their releases in both her orifices. Obscene, being used like this, but she accepted it, relished it, loved it. She loved it. Shamelessly, blissfully, and utterly loved it.

Malcolm pulled out first, and Mona sat up with the midnight man still inside her.

"Beautiful," he said as she arched her back and shook out her hair. "Why are you only a dream?"

"I'm not," she said.

He raised his head and whispered into her ear, "I wish I could believe that." She only laughed. Mona knew just how he felt. He rolled them over onto her back and slid out of her. She closed her eyes and stretched out in the dappled sunlight streaming through the tree canopy overhead. The stream babbled and bubbled in the near distance. Her thighs were slick with semen and she couldn't stop smiling.

"Are you happy?" Malcolm asked. She opened her eyes and nodded.

"And messy," she said, spreading her legs to show him how wet they'd made her.

"Oh dear. We'll have to do something about that, won't we?" Malcolm asked. He turned to the man with the midnight eyes. "What do you think?"

"I think…" the midnight man began. "I think…you're too slow, old man!"

At that, the midnight man stripped and ran naked to the water.

"Lads," Malcolm said, shaking his head. "They never do grow up."

"Never," Mona said. Malcolm stripped naked as quickly as the midnight man and she had no choice but to chase after them as to the stream. She ran freely, fearlessly, knowing this world was safe for her. Her feet would strike no stones. No snakes were hidden in the grass.

She reached the stream and stood atop a large flat rock at the water's edge. The midnight man had caught the bathing woman in his arms. He ripped the wet and clinging muslin fabric off her body. She laughed and squirmed happily in his grasp and put up no fight whatsoever to flee his attentions. Malcolm stood on the rock next to her and dove into the water, his long lean body as agile and muscled as a man half his age. She sat on the rock and let her legs dangle into the water as Malcolm swam back to her. He stood at the stream's edge, submerged from the waist down, and she let him lift her into the water. The water was warm as bathwater and she eagerly wrapped her legs around Malcolm's back and her arms around his shoulders. He pushed his cock into her. It went in easily as she was still so open from earlier. She sighed and rested her head on Malcolm's strong shoulder.

They didn't speak and didn't kiss. They merely rested together in the water, their bodies intimately intertwined. She half dozed, half watched as Malcolm's friend coupled with the bathing woman in the shallow waters. He had her bent backward over a smooth log of driftwood while he fondled her ample breasts. He pinched and pulled the nipples, sucked the tender pink tips, all the while the woman moaned in her pleasure.

"Who is he?" Mona asked.

"A dear friend."

"Is he real?"

"As real as I am."

"Are you real?"

"You ask many questions for a woman who cares so little for the answers."

"I'm afraid of losing you," she said. "That's all."

"You'll always have me with you, if you wish," he said.

"You know I wish it."

"Then it will be so."

She needed no other consolation. Those were the words she'd wanted for weeks. Under the stream's surface, Malcolm was fucking her again, using the weightlessness of the water to lift her up by the waist and slide her down onto him. As he took her, she watched the bathing woman and the midnight man. He'd pulled her to the very edge of the stream where the water was only a few inches deep and put her on her hands and knees. Mona watched as the midnight man mounted her from behind, his hands gripping her waist to steady himself. It was mesmerizing, watching him take her. Mona watched the muscles of his thighs and buttocks contract and flex with his thrusts. She watched his thick red cock pushing into her body with the steady rhythm of a piston. A beautiful man, broad-shouldered and lean but with muscle enough to do real damage if he wanted. She could have watched him all day.

"Mona…" Malcolm whispered her name into her ear. He was coming, she could tell from the tautness of his body and how hard he held her to him. When it was over he tilted her back and let her float on the surface of the stream, her candy apple hair an icon's halo around her head. Malcolm gently played with her naked breasts as she lay on the water with her legs still wrapped around his waist. There was nothing she wouldn't allow him to do to her body and she told him that.

"I'm glad to hear it," he said as he tugged lightly on her nipples. "I fully intend to use your body."

"For what?" she asked, not that it mattered. It was all the same to her. If Malcolm was doing the using, her body was his plaything.

"I told you. To keep a promise I made."

"When will you keep it?" She smiled up at the bare sun overhead. This was heaven. This was bliss. This was everything she'd been too afraid to dream but would have dreamed if she'd dared.

Malcolm cradled her head in his hand and lifted her out of the water, bringing her face to face with him. He kissed her on the mouth, a deep velvety kiss. Their tongues met and mingled as the water lapped and licked her skin. At the stream's shore, the midnight man was still copulating with the beautiful black-haired woman who now lay on her back, her ankles in the air as the midnight man pummeled her with brutal thrusts. With one hard push, Malcolm penetrated Mona again, right into the core of her and when she gasped from the sudden intrusion, he smiled and answered her question.

"I shall start to keep it…now."

Mona's eyes flew open. She lay on the bed in the back room and though she was all alone, her body shook with an orgasm. Her fingers slid inside her wetness, that tight inner ring of muscles spasming around her own hand.

When it passed, she rolled onto her side into the fetal position. Malcolm had never left her like this before, never this suddenly, never while she was awake. It scared her. But she saw a white envelope on the pillow next to her and sat up in excitement. Perhaps he hadn't left her alone after all.

In her haste to open the envelope, she cut her finger on the fine paper and soon the white was dotted with red. She didn't care. She cared only for the words she devoured, the words written in Malcolm's loping handwriting.

 Mona, my darling whore,

You don't know what a gift you've given me this past year. Although I have paid for it and paid for

it dearly, it was well worth the price. I know now all will be as I wished it to be.

Someone is coming for me. I owe him a debt and as you know all too well, debts must be paid. But he kept his end of the bargain and it's my turn to keep mine. As for our bargain, I admit I didn't tell you the entire truth at our second meeting when I said you were sitting on a goldmine. You thought I referred to your body and in a way I did. What I should have said was you are sleeping on a goldmine. Open the bed knobs and you will see what I mean.

As for who I am, you will know it soon enough.

All my lust,

Malcolm

P.S. Do anything you must, but keep me forever.

The bed knobs? What on earth did he mean by "open the bed knobs"? And what on earth did he mean by keep him forever? Surely that was his responsibility, not hers. The tone of the note unnerved her greatly. Something about it seemed final. Something about it seemed like a goodbye.

Mona stood and stared at the bed knobs. The one closest to her at the foot of the bed was nothing more than a brass ball. She put her hand on the knob and turned it. At first it didn't want to give, but then she felt it twist the tiniest bit. With both hands she turned the knob again. The old bed didn't want to let the knob go, but eventually she managed to take the knob off. She looked inside the post and found that while it was hollow as she would have expected, it was not empty.

Something was inside it. Something rolled up and wrapped in yellowing linen. Carefully she extracted the linen tube from inside the bedpost. She took the linen wrapping off and discovered a rolled canvas beneath it. Mona shook as she unfurled the canvas, going slowly as she could to avoid doing any damage to the painting that had been hidden in her bed for God only knew how long. At first she saw nothing but black. Then a bit of red on either side. A pocket with a gold chain. Then buttons followed by a white collar. Then a face she knew better than her own, a devilishly handsome face, not smiling at the mouth but a little in the eyes, the eyes that were so black one couldn't tell where the pupil ended and the iris began.

Malcolm in a black three-piece suit. That was the painting. At the bottom of the canvas was a name of a portrait painter she recognized at once, because they'd had an exhibition of his portraits of women at The Red Gallery five years ago. A man famous for his paintings of England's high society. A man who had been dead since the 1950s.

Mona turned the painting over.

It couldn't be. No. It couldn't.

And yet, there it was, written in pencil on the back of the canvas.

Portrait in oil, 1938.

XI: THE RAPE OF THE SABINE
WOMEN

Three months later

"The *Times* called again," Gabrielle said as she stood in the doorway of Mona's office.

"What do they want this time?" Mona asked, barely glancing up from her auction catalog.

"They say they wish to run a feature on the gallery for the Society page. I think you should do it, yes?"

Mona looked up at her assistant. Gabrielle was tall and shapely and black and had the loveliest French accent that made every word sound like it had been dipped in silver. "Society" was *Zociety* and "yes" was *yezz*. The combination of her beauty and her accent had made Gabrielle the perfect hire for The Red. No one could tell this woman no when she said, "You wish to buy it, of course. I will wrap it up for you."

"I suppose we ought to say yes," Mona said. "The *Times* has given us good free press."

"I'll call them and let them know tomorrow morning. It's good to let both men and newspapers sweat a little before you tell them yes."

"Good advice," Mona said. Gabrielle smiled and strode from the doorway in her black suit and towering black high heels. It was so nice to be able to afford employees again. Since the discovery of the paintings rolled up and hidden in the brass bed, The Red Gallery's telephone had been ringing day and night with buyers, reporters, and all the curious. Mona had found two paintings hidden in the bedposts, though the art world only knew of one—a lost Picasso, a painting of one of his many mistresses. The second painting she told no one about. She'd had it framed and hung in a place of honor in The Red Gallery with a tag that read "*Unknown Man*, 1938, artist Anthony Devas."

The Picasso she'd had authenticated, and, despite the lack of provenance, the art world had gone mad over it. Mona had lent it to an art museum which could provide the best security, cleaning, and crowds to see it. She was entertaining offers from buyers for the Picasso and all the sketches and etchings Malcolm had given her, but she didn't want to sell them quite yet. The Picasso had been Malcolm's parting gift to her. Since he'd left her without giving her the child she'd wanted from him, she was reluctant to give up anything associated with him. Every single day she thought of him. She woke up remembering him. She fell asleep and dreamt of him. She pleasured herself fantasizing of him. And every day she came to The Red, unlocked the door, pushed back the curtains, and stared into his dark smiling eyes that stared back at her from inside the gilt frame. She'd hung the portrait of Malcolm where she'd once hung *The Fox Hunt* by Morland. In her mind, Malcolm was standing there staring at that painting, one hand on his hip, the other on his chin. In her heart, he would always be there. It was in her body where she wanted him, but that wasn't possible. If Malcolm had been forty or so in 1938, then he would be over one hundred now, making it unlikely he was still alive. Had it been his ghost that had come to her? Had he somehow traveled through time, or otherwise found a way into her in dreams? She didn't know; she would, most likely, never know. But he'd kept one part of his promise. He'd saved The Red. After the Picasso had been appraised in the millions of dollars, the collections agencies had stopped calling. The bank restructured her loan and she'd been able to take out a line of credit again, hire Gabrielle, have the gallery painted and repaired, and once more the art world was calling. She should have been so happy...

And yet.

Malcolm.

He'd said she could keep him and so she had. She kept him in a frame on the wall. It wasn't what she wanted, but it would have to do, wouldn't it?

Mona sighed. A tear fell from her eye and landed onto the auction catalog. Silly girl, crying over a man who'd paid her to have sex with him. Nonsense. She should act like the grown woman she was and not a lovesick schoolgirl. She yanked open her desk drawer to fetch a tissue and found a book of art she didn't recall putting in there. She took it out and found a page marked with a red velvet ribbon.

Malcolm?

She couldn't breathe. She had to force herself to inhale and exhale as she extracted the book from inside the drawer and laid it atop her desk. She opened the page to the ribbon and gasped.

A Rubens painting. *The Rape of the Sabine Women*, 1637.

Shivering in fear and shock, Mona stared at the famous painting. She knew it well. They'd studied it in one of her many art history courses. The painting, a riot of movement and color and light, depicted the famous abduction of the daughters of the Sabine men who had refused to allow the Roman men to marry into their families. Mona's mother had hated that the word *raptio*—meaning "abduction"—was translated into English as "rape." She said it made the women sound like victims, when in fact they bravely intervened during the subsequent war between the Sabines and the Romans to put a stop to the killing of their husbands by their fathers and the killing of their fathers by their husbands. But that was the sort of thing her mother would take issue with. Mona had reminded her that even if they hadn't been raped, they had been kidnapped and forced into marriage. Her mother waved the objection off and told Mona they'd been veritable prisoners of their fathers anyway, so it wasn't as if life was sunshine and roses before they were abducted. Mona accused her mother of applying her "beauty over truth" standard to history. Her mother had only scoffed and said, "You've never heard of the Holy Sabine Empire, have you? The Romans won for a reason." Mona had let the subject drop and had given the painting little thought since then.

Until now.

Mona rose from her chair and ran to the back room. She threw open the door and found...nothing. Nothing but paintings, sculptures, boxes, and supplies. Mona had moved the brass bed to her apartment. The back room was nothing but storage now. Malcolm certainly wasn't there. She'd half-expected to find him in a Roman centurion's uniform ready to throw her over his horse's saddle and ride off with her to his home where he would make her his wife. A nice fantasy, but only a fantasy.

Someone was playing a cruel trick on her. Mona closed the door to the back room behind her.

"I'll lock up now if you like," Gabrielle said in the office doorway.

"Yes, thank you," Mona said.

"Are you working late again?"

"Always."

"You work too much," Gabrielle said. "You should take time off. You know I can watch The Red for you and Tou-Tou. You haven't taken a day off since I started."

Mona smiled. Gabrielle was kind and they got along well, but Mona had never worked up the courage to tell her lovely assistant that she came to The Red every day because of Malcolm—because she missed him, because she was certain he wasn't quite done with her yet. How do you tell a woman as rational and intelligent as Gabrielle that you were in love with a man who was most likely a ghost? You didn't, of course. So Mona kept her secrets to herself.

"I'll think about that," Mona said. Perhaps she would take some time off. She couldn't be held hostage by a memory all her life, could she? "Although I don't know what I'd do with myself."

"You will figure that out." Gabrielle turned to leave. "Or not."

"I won't figure it out?"

"No, I won't lock up." Gabrielle looked at Mona over her shoulder. "He's still here."

She whispered the last words and Mona narrowed her eyes at her assistant. Gabrielle crooked her finger at Mona and Mona walked over to the door.

"Who is that?" Gabrielle whispered. "He's been here for over an hour." Mona peered into the gallery. A man stood in front of the portrait of Malcolm, one hand on his hip, the other in his pocket. "Tou-Tou likes him."

The little black cat sat on the floor at the man's feet. They both seemed to be staring at the painting.

"I don't know," Mona said.

"He's terribly handsome," Gabrielle whispered.

Mona couldn't deny it. She straightened her red skirt and black blouse. "You can go out the side door," Mona said. "I'll lock up after he's gone."

Gabrielle smiled. She unbuttoned one button on Mona's blouse, revealing the lace edge of her black bra.

"You'll thank me later," Gabrielle said before leaving Mona all alone in the gallery with the man in the suit.

After Gabrielle was gone and the gallery empty but for her, Tou-Tou, and the man, Mona forced herself to go out to him. She almost buttoned her blouse up again but didn't. Why bother?

"Sir? We're closing," she said. The man didn't look at her, nor acknowledge that she'd spoken. He had reddish brown hair, wavy and rakish, and his eyes were very dark...but unmistakably blue. Midnight blue. Lean but broad-shouldered, strong nose and strong chin and strong jaw, he was more handsome than any man had a right to be.

He looked very familiar to her, but she couldn't quite place him.

"Sir?"

"I need to speak to the owner of this establishment," the man said in a crisp English accent.

"I'm Mona St. James. I'm the owner."

"Well, Miss St. James, how much for the painting?"

"It's not for sale," she said.

"Everything is for sale. Name your price, I'll pay it."

"This painting is priceless."

He scoffed. "Priceless? I refuse to believe it means anything to you. You don't even know who he is, do you? Besides, your card is wrong."

"I disagree," she said. "My assistant is very thorough in her research. The painting is clearly marked 1938 and the artist is undoubtedly Anthony Devas."

"That's not what's incorrect. The subject of the painting is the problem. He's not an 'unknown man.' I know that because I know him."

"You know him?"

"His name is Malcolm Arthur Augustus Fitzroy, thirteenth Earl of Godwick."

Mona covered her mouth with her fingers, silencing her gasp. Finally. At last. She knew his name. Malcolm Arthur Augustus Fitzroy. The Earl of Godwick.

"You know this for certain?"

"I know this for certain," the man said.

"How?"

He turned and looked at her directly in the face. He had a commanding air to him. Commanding and powerful. A man used to having his way.

"Because my name is Spencer Arthur Malcolm Fitzroy, and I'm the fifteenth Earl of Godwick. That 'unknown' man on your wall is my grandfather."

"Malcolm is your grandfather?"

"He was, yes. Although he died long before I was born." The man's handsome brow furrowed. "Did you say your name was Mona?"

"Yes," she said. "You're Malcolm's grandson." She knew she was repeating herself, but she was in too much shock to stay silent.

"How did you come across this painting?" the Earl asked.

"How did you know I had it?" she asked.

"I asked you first."

"I won't answer until you answer," she said.

"The *Sunday Times* had an article about a lost Picasso painting found in America. A painting of a woman in red and blue. There was also a photograph of the interior of The Red, with a familiar painting in the background...a painting that once hung in Wingthorn Hall, my family's ancestral home."

"I found it rolled up in the post of my bed," she said.

"A brass bed. An antique brass bed."

"Yes, it is. But how—" She hadn't told the newspapers the bed was brass. She'd only said "my mother's old bed."

"My grandfather was the last of the great English rakes. His sexual appetite was legendary and his prowess even more so. He refused to marry, to settle down, to do his duty by his name and family. Instead he spent nearly every night in brothels with 'his darling whores,' as he called them. That's all he spent his money on—prostitutes and art."

"I can think of worse ways to waste one's fortune."

"Hardly wasted. The art he purchased saved the family fortune. The economy was in tatters after the war. But art—great art—always goes up in value. Only the Queen has more money than we do now."

"Malcolm was a very wise man then. And I have to admire an art lover."

"Oh, he was an art lover, all right. He and his girls would put on plays for the other brothel patrons. They'd reenact scenes from paintings, the more erotic the better. His exploits were legendary. Not too many earls performed in near-public orgies."

"A pity," Mona said. "They should have."

"Yes, a pity indeed. The family was always trying to tame him. Just when they thought he'd settled down after he turned forty, he fell madly in lust with an eighteen-year-old prostitute named Mona Blessey. He showered her with gifts."

"Art," Mona said.

"Art, indeed." The Earl nodded. "Sketches—Degas among them. Paintings, including the Picasso you found. And even his own official portrait he ripped off the wall in Wingthorn. At age forty-one, he finally gave in to his mother's begging and married a girl with no money who would put up with his rakish ways and not make too much of a fuss. The very day he learned she was pregnant, he left her for Mona. An Earl's wife is a countess. My rather foul-mouthed grandfather called Mona his—"

"His cuntess," Mona said.

"Exactly. How did you know?"

"An educated guess. Go on."

"When Mona Blessey's father learned where they were holed up, he traveled to Scotland and found my grandfather in his daughter's bed. He ordered my grandfather to return to his wife and unborn child in England and let his daughter go. My grandfather refused. So the man shot him."

"In the chest," Mona said, remembering her dream of *The Bleeding Man*.

"Yes, in the chest," the Earl said. "Do you know—"

"Keep talking. Tell me everything."

"He bled out quickly, but he lived long enough to cough out his last words to her father. He said, 'If I must sell my soul to the devil to do it, I will find a way back into Mona's bed. A whore will reign as Countess of Godwick. You'll see...'"

The Earl paused. "He died laughing in Mona Blessey's arms."

Mona turned her back on the Earl. She covered her face with her hands and breathed.

"Hounded by reporters and vilified in the papers, Mona Blessey left for America the very next week. She had the bed my grandfather died in shipped along with her things. I thought that sounded awfully sentimental for a teenage prostitute. I should have known she was using the bed to smuggle the artwork out of the country. Somehow that bed ended up in your possession."

"My mother bought it nearly thirty years ago at an estate sale. She told me that's where my name came from—Mona was the name of the woman who'd owned the bed. Mother said she'd been a courtesan in her youth, and I didn't believe it. Mother could stretch the truth every now and then. But in this case she was right, wasn't she?"

"She was," the Earl said. "And now you know the story of

the painting. It belongs to my family. I'll have to ask you to return it."

"No," she said, facing him.

"No? No isn't an option. It's my family's painting."

"It's my painting. Malcolm was the rightful owner and gave it to Mona Blessey. Mona put it in her bedpost for safe-keeping. My mother bought the bed. I was conceived in the bed your grandfather died in. The bed is legally mine. The painting was in the bed and therefore the painting is mine and always will be. No court of law in America or the United Kingdom would disagree. And you know it," she said. "Otherwise you wouldn't have asked me how much I was willing to sell it for."

"I was hoping to avoid a legal battle."

"I'll allow a professional to make a copy of the painting, if you like. But the painting is mine."

"He's my grandfather, not yours. He's nothing to you."

"He's not nothing to me, not by any stretch of the imagination. You've never met him."

"Neither have you."

"I know him," she said. She walked to the painting of Malcolm and stood before it, staring into his gleaming dark eyes. He'd told her of a deathbed promise and that she was his way of fulfilling it. How could she have known it was his own deathbed promise he spoke of? Her mother had named her after Mona Blessey, the whore he'd loved. She'd been conceived in that bed, had slept in it all her life. She'd lost her virginity in that bed and had taken Ryan's there years later. All the while Malcolm's spirit or soul or whatever it was that survived his death, was tied to that bed or perhaps tied to the painting in the bed. When the time came when she was at her most desperate, her most vulnerable, her most willing to sell herself to save The Red, Malcolm came to her in the flesh even though he'd been dead for decades. He'd come to her in the flesh because he'd sold his soul to the devil to do it. And the devil had smirked, not smiled, because the devil does not smile.

"Malcolm…" she breathed.

The Earl came to stand behind her. She felt uncomfortably aware of his body so close to hers, the subtle heat of him, his looming height, the power of him barely restrained by a suit and good breeding.

"You know him," he said. "You mean that, don't you?"

"I do."

"Dreams?"

She turned and faced him. "Something like that."

He sighed, nodded. "I have them too. Sometimes I think I'm losing my mind, they're so vivid, so powerful."

"Malcolm comes to you in your dreams?"

"Once a year. At most twice a year. We talk. He…guides me, I suppose you could say. He says I take after him. I shouldn't take that as a compliment but I do. Two years ago I almost married someone, and I had a dream that the old Earl told me not to do it. We broke up and later I found she had only pretended to be in love with me. She wanted the title, not me. He saved me from a bad marriage—all from within a dream."

Mona remembered something Malcolm had told her, that he was fond only of his youngest offspring, the one who took after him. That had to be the Earl. Spencer Arthur Malcolm Fitzroy, the youngest child in his bloodline.

"Another time…" The Earl's voice trailed off. "I can't remember much of the dream. But there was a girl in it with hair as red as fire and apples. Like yours."

So that was why he seemed so familiar. The Earl of Godwick—this arrogant man—was her dream lover, the man with the midnight eyes. He looked different without the beard, but it was him. Right here before her in the flesh, with blue eyes so dark and cold that she shivered as if submerged in the deepest coldest ocean.

"They're only dreams," he said, and it sounded as if he were telling that to himself, that he needed to believe they were only dreams when he knew otherwise.

"Not only," Mona said. "Not only dreams."

"Don't say such things," he snapped.

"If you insist." She could have told him more. She could have recounted their "luncheon on the grass" together; she could have told him about her other nights with Malcolm, and the all too real stains on the sheets every morning after. But no. A serious, stern man like the Earl would probably go mad to know that life and death weren't as absolute as they seemed.

"I have to have the painting," he said. "I simply have to have it. There is a blank space on the wall that's been waiting since 1938 for my grandfather to come home. I won't leave here without him."

"You'll have to. The painting is mine. He wanted me to have it."

"You say these dreams are more than dreams? Tell me then why in my last dream of him, he made me promise that I would do anything to bring it home? Anything."

"I'm afraid Malcolm is playing one last little trick on us." She sympathized with the Earl, but Malcolm had told her to keep the painting, no matter what.

"Any price."

"I won't sell it," she said. "It's mine. It goes where I go and that's the end of it. I'm sorry, but my decision is final. If you want to sue me for the painting, you may. I'll win, but if you feel you must, you must."

"You have no idea how much money I could pay you for that painting."

"This has nothing to do with money. I have a Picasso in

my possession that's been appraised for thirteen million dollars. And now that you've given me impeccable provenance, it will fetch even more."

"I could give you more than thirteen million dollars for my grandfather's painting."

"I told you, it's not about the money. No amount of money in the world would buy that painting from me. It's not for sale. As we say in this country, sir, no means no."

The Earl seemed to ponder that for a good long time. Mona meant every word. Had he pulled out his wallet and written her a check for one hundred billion dollars she would have torn it into pieces and scattered it on the floor like confetti.

"It goes where you go," the Earl said.

"As I said, I won't part with the painting as long as I live. And I plan on living a good long life."

"I see." He put his hand on his hip again, his other hand on his chin. He stared at Malcolm and Malcolm returned the gaze. "There's a story they tell of him in the family, one we have never made public. Mona Blessey wasn't a prostitute. She was the respectable daughter of the family steward—respectable until my grandfather took an interest in her, that was. One night her father lost everything at the card tables, ruining the family and Mona's prospects for marriage. My grandfather offered to make her his mistress. She warned him her father would kill him if they were caught together. My grandfather kidnapped her anyway and spirited her off to Scotland."

"Why do I think she didn't put up much of a fight?"

"Because you know my grandfather. His 'victim' had her bags packed the night he stole her out of her bed. He did whatever he wanted and cared nothing for what anyone thought of him. He died laughing in his lover's bed. He took what he wanted and asked no man's permission. What a way to live. A better way to die. Wouldn't you agree?"

"Yes," she said. "The world needs more men like Malcolm, more women like Mona Blessey."

"I'm glad to hear you say that," he said. "I couldn't agree more."

The Earl stepped forward and plucked Malcolm's painting off the wall. Mona lunged forward to rescue it but the Earl wrapped his other arm around her hips, hoisted her over his shoulder, and carried her out of the gallery and into the back seat of a long black town car waiting in the alley out back.

"You planned to steal my painting, didn't you?" Mona demanded as he threw her down onto the supple leather seats.

"It was Plan B," he said. Then he called up to the chauffeur with a haughty "Drive."

"You could be arrested for this," she said.

The car rolled out of the alley and onto the street. She tried the doors but they were all locked. Mona knew she should have been panicking, but she wasn't afraid at all. Only furious.

"Arrested? For what? For eloping? It's not a crime. Would you rather be married in Scotland or America? I'll let you make that decision. Marriage, I hear, is all about compromise."

He propped the painting up on the bench seat across from them. If it were possible—and now she believed anything was—Malcolm's eyes seemed to be laughing.

"Married? Have you lost your mind?"

"Only my inhibitions," he said. "And you did say the painting goes where you go and that you'd never sell it. If we marry, it becomes half mine. And half is better than nothing.

You'll love Wingthorn. The most beautiful home in the country. Lady Mona has a nice ring to it, doesn't it?"

"Look, Lord Godwick or whoever the hell you are—"

"Call me Spencer, love. We are going to be married, after all."

"Turn this car around right now and take me back to my gallery, *Spencer*."

"You can return to the gallery once we're married. If you wish. Although I'd rather keep you at Wingthorn with me. Ever seen a Wingthorn rose? White petals, red thorns big as knife points. Beautiful and dangerous, my favorite combination."

"The minute you turn your back on me I'm calling the police," Mona said.

"I won't turn my back then," he said. "I'd rather look at you anyway."

He raised his hand to touch her face, and she tried to slap it away. He caught her by the wrist and yanked her to him, capturing her in his arms and holding her against his chest.

"Aren't you a darling," he said as he subdued her with his vastly superior physical strength. He clasped the back of her neck with his hand and she gave up the fight. He looked at her face, at her lips, at her neck. In her struggle against him, her blouse had opened, revealing the swell of her breasts. Gently he touched her panting chest with his fingertips. "How old are you?"

"Twenty-six," she said.

"I'm thirty-seven. Time to settle down, I've been told."

"This is how you settle down? By kidnapping me and forcing me to marry you for a painting? I won't do it. I have a cat to take care of."

"Surely your exquisite assistant can care for him until we can bring him over. I like pussies of all varieties. He'll be our little lord of the manor."

"I don't even have my passport, you bastard."

"We'll go and fetch it." He lowered the window an inch between the back seat and the front. "Driver? Swing up by Miss St. James's flat." He rolled the window back up again and smiled at her. "Not a problem."

"You're mad."

"And you're lovely when you're furious. I can't wait to make you furious for years and years to come."

"Take me back to the gallery this instant. I will not marry you."

"Won't you?" he asked, tilting his head to the side, his tone taunting.

"Never," she said.

"Most women of my acquaintance would kill to be a wealthy countess."

"Marry one of them then."

He traced the lace at the edge of her bra and her skin prickled with pleasure.

"Where's the fun in marrying someone who wants to marry you? I prefer a challenge."

"I'm a person, not a challenge. This isn't a game."

"It is a game, and I'm going to win. See?" He pressed his lips to hers and she pushed back away from him, or tried to. He let her go only so far before he forced her to return the kiss. With his hand on the nape of her neck and his other arm pinning her against him, she could do nothing but surrender to the kiss.

But she refused to enjoy it.

Spencer lips moved over hers with surprising softness that left her breathless and warm. His tongue darted out from his mouth and licked the bow of her bottom lip. It shocked her into opening her mouth and the second she did, his tongue slipped inside. His mouth was hot against her and insistent. Every time his tongue touched hers, a current of pure erotic electricity shot through her body and into her loins. She tried to hate him and hate the kiss and hate what was happening to her, and perhaps she would have had she never known and loved Malcolm. But he'd trained her to submit to the lusts of powerful men. Trained her to do it and trained her to like it. No, not to like it. He'd trained her to love it. She hated Spencer, this arrogant Earl who acted as if he already owned her. But she couldn't hate his kisses, try as she might. God help her, she might even love them.

Spencer reached into her blouse and slid his hand under the lace cup of her bra. He found her nipple and pinched it lightly. She flinched and her nipple hardened instantly. Spencer chuckled softly at her arousal and she tried to push away from him again.

"Oh no, you're not going anywhere," he said, pinching the nipple again, harder this time. She struggled against him again but Spencer was far too strong. He pushed the lace cup down, baring her breast. She stilled in his inescapable grasp. He looked down at her breast, caressed the soft flesh and smiled. He lowered his head and licked her nipple before taking it into his hot mouth.

Mona's head fell back in ecstasy but Spencer caught her and held her against his shoulder. As he suckled her breast, he slid his hand under her skirt, found the edge of her black panties and pulled them down. He brought his hand between her thighs, cupped her sex, and inserted a finger into her. He moaned softly against her body. She was wet inside and burning hot. He pushed a second finger in, a third, and all the way up to the knuckles. He fucked her with his hand as he sucked her nipple and there was nothing she could do but take it. He was going to make her orgasm, force her to orgasm. She didn't want to, she didn't. Once she did she would be his, all his, forever his.

"The things I will do to you..." he murmured against her skin.

"What things?"

"I'll keep you a naked slave chained to my bed. I'll show off your cunt to every man who crosses the threshold of my house so they can see my prized possession and envy me. I will fuck beautiful women in front of you and send them home right after, still dripping my seed, so you will know that I can have any girl I want but you, you'll be the only one I'll keep. I will tie you to the dining room table and drink my wine out of you. I'll let my dearest friends bend you over the billiard table and fuck your pussy and arse while I sit in my favorite club chair, sipping Scotch and watching you writhe for my entertainment. Then later when I'm fucking you in our bed, you will tell me in exquisite detail how much you prefer my cock to theirs. You're a magnificent whore and I will wrap you around my cock every day for the rest of your life..."

Mona couldn't hold back anymore. She came with a cry, muscles going wild all around Spencer's fingers buried deep inside her. He swore violently as she came, seemingly shocked by the force of her orgasm. Slowly her eyes opened and she looked at him, blinking and spent.

"Scotland," she said. "Let's be married in Scotland."

Her mother would have approved this match.

"Lovely little girl," Spencer said, smiling. "Though it'll kill me, I won't stick my cock in you until after the ceremony if only so we can tell our children someday how their mother and father waited till marriage. They won't need to know I kidnapped you and forced you to marry me the day we met."

"Our little secret," she said. She would never tell Spencer they'd met once before, made love once before. To him it was nothing but a dream, but she knew. She and Malcolm knew. Their little secret...

"You're going to make me a marvelous countess, I can already tell," he said, tenderly caressing her swollen clitoris under her skirt. "A fine lady by day, a better whore by night. My whore."

"Your whore," she said, sighing. Spencer kissed her again and she let him. Why not? She was his now and always would be. This is what Malcolm planned, this is what he wanted to bring about, and in a day or two it would be done. Malcolm wanted her to have his heir, he had said, and now she would indeed have his heir—she would have Spencer for a husband and Spencer would have her for his lover and his slave. She would have Spencer's children, the next heirs. And Mona, the whore, would reign as the Countess of Godwick.

From inside his frame, the portrait of Malcolm smiled.

Or was it a smirk?

The End.

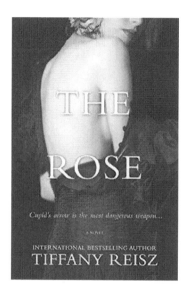

USA Today **bestselling author Tiffany Reisz returns to the world of *The Red* with an imaginative sequel full of lust and magic, and the dangers unleashed when the two are combined . . .**

On the day of Lia's university graduation party, her parents —wealthy art collectors with friends in high places—gift her a beautiful wine cup, a rare artifact known as the Rose *kylix*. It was used in the temple ceremonies of Eros, Greek god of erotic love, and has the power to bring the most intimate sexual fantasies to life. When Lia drinks from it, she is suddenly immersed in an erotic myth so vivid it seems real...

ABOUT THE AUTHOR

Tiffany Reisz is the USA Today-bestselling author of the Romance Writers of America RITA®-winning Original Sinners series from Harlequin's Mira Books. Tiffany lives in Louisville, Kentucky with her husband, author Andrew Shaffer, and two cats. The cats are not writers.

Visit Tiffany's website to subscribe to her e-mail newsletter. Subscribers receive a free eBook copy of Something Nice, *a standalone novella set in Tiffany's Original Sinners universe:* www.tiffanyreisz.com/mailing-list

facebook.com/littleredridingcrop
goodreads.com/tiffanyreisz
instagram.com/tiffany_reisz

In his three years working as a Jack-of-All-Wicked-Trades for an unnamed underground network, Lieutenant Kingsley Boissonneault has done it all—spied, lied, and killed under orders. But his latest assignment is quite out of the ordinary. His commanding officer's nephew has disappeared inside a sex cult, and Kingsley has been tasked with bringing him home to safety. Once inside the Chateau, however, Kingsley quickly falls under the spell cast by the enigmatic Madame, a woman of wisdom, power, and beauty.

"A surprisingly engrossing erotic thriller . . ."
— *The New York Times Book Review*

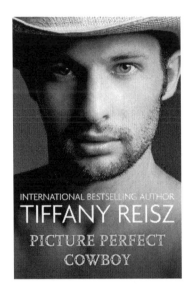

Jason "Still" Waters' life looks perfect from the outside—
money, fame, and the words "World Champion Bull-Rider"
after his name. But Jason has a secret, one he never planned
on telling anybody . . . until he meets Simone. She's the kinky
girl of his dreams . . . and his conservative family's worst
nightmare.

"Blazingly erotic."
— *Publishers Weekly*

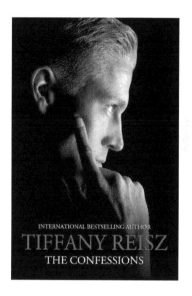

Father Stuart Ballard has been Marcus Stearns' confessor since the young Jesuit was only eighteen years old. He thought he'd heard every sin the boy had to confess until Marcus uttered those three fateful words: "I met Eleanor."

So begins "The Confession of Marcus Stearns," a moving coda to the RITA® Award-winning Original Sinners series.

"This is the reward for the tempestuous journey of all those who have read the series . . ."
— Heroes & Heartbreakers

MICHAEL'S
WINGS
AN ORIGINAL SINNERS COLLECTION

TIFFANY REISZ

A companion collection to *The Angel,* featuring a new novella and five previously-published short stories starring the Original Sinners' Michael and Griffin.

Stories include "Griffin in Wonderland," "Gauze," "The Theory of the Moment," "A Better Distraction," "Christmas in Suite 37A," and a brand new erotic novella guest-starring Mistress Nora!

"Trademark Tiffany Reisz . . . I loved every minute of it."
— TotallyBooked

Printed in Great Britain
by Amazon